DAUGHTERS OF THE MOON

possession

Also in the
DAUGHTERS OF THE MOON
series:

DAUGHTERS OF THE MOON

possession

LYNNE EWING

HYPERION/NEW YORK

Copyright © 2002 by Lynne Ewing

Volo and the Volo colophon are trademarks of Disney Enterprises, Inc.
All rights reserved. No part of this book may be reproduced or transmitted in any
form or by any means, electronic or mechanical, including photocopying, recording, or
by any information storage and retrieval system, without written permission from the
publisher. For information address Volo Books, 114 Fifth Avenue, New York,
New York 10011-5690.

First Edition
5 7 9 10 8 6
Printed in the United States of America

Library of Congress Cataloging-in-Publication Data on file.

ISBN 0-7868-0850-0 (hc)

Visit www.volobooks.com

For Marti Brooks of Idaho Falls, and
Vanessa Renee Gallegos

—⟡⟡⟡—

With many thanks to Andrea Brooks,
Laura Brooks, Husnah Khan, Andrew
Mayesh, Sami Mayesh, and, of course,
my wonderful editor Alessandra Balzer

I n A.D. 1223 an infant was born, clutching a jewel in her tiny fist. Her peasant father ran to the castle to bring back a priest, but by the time they returned to the hut, the jewel had disappeared. The priest declared that such would be the child's life: all good would slip through her fingers.

The years passed, and the girl's beauty became celebrated. Knights and kings journeyed far to gaze into her eyes before leaving on their crusades. Women and children made pilgrimages to look upon her angelic face. All who saw her felt blessed.

But an ancient evil called the Atrox also saw her unearthly perfection and pursued her, offering her father great treasures if she would betroth it. The girl saw her father's poverty and agreed to the union, making only one request for herself—that her beauty should last forever. The Atrox agreed, and she pledged her devotion for eternity.

A Follower of the Atrox came to take the young woman to the underworld, but when he saw her beauty and grace, he fell desperately in love with her and she, too, with him.

They tried to hide their love, but the Atrox saw through their deception. When the young woman stepped into the Cold Fire to receive immortality, instead of preserving her beauty for eternity, the flames consumed her flesh and bones, turning her into a wind spirit.

The knight could not endure life without her. The force of his love drove him across the world, searching for a sorceress with the power to restore her human form. As he was crossing the sea, a storm broke out and sent his ship off course to the island of Aeaea, where Circe, an ancient enchantress, lived. Circe gave him a magic potion. With it, his beloved could possess any body she desired.

Since then many young women have felt her presence and wondered afterward what made them act so wickedly, never understanding that for a brief time, the spirit of the wind had taken over their mind and soul.

CHAPTER ONE

SERENA RAN TOWARD the bus stop, bumping through the late-afternoon shoppers on Melrose Avenue. The smells of frying garlic spun around her, making her anxious to be home. She hadn't eaten all day. Maybe that was why she felt so edgy and on the verge of tears. She glanced at the sidewalk diners. She could almost taste the linguine on the plates of the first table.

The squeal of brakes made her turn. Her bus was rolling to the curb. She couldn't miss it. Her fingers already ached from carrying her cello case, and her back hurt from the heavy load of books in her messenger bag. She started to shove through four breathless girls peering into a psychic's shop.

"That's him!" the first one squealed, and stepped back, starstruck, blocking Serena's way.

Serena pressed around her, but the second girl leaned forward for a better look inside, blocking her path again.

"I heard he always comes down here to have his fortune read," the one wearing blue lipstick whispered.

The bus doors swooshed open, and passengers began boarding, tossing money in the fare box and grabbing hand straps.

"Excuse me," Serena said with rising frustration.

The girls broke apart, creating a narrow space between them.

Serena squeezed forward, her cello case poised in front of her, and paused.

Jerome was waiting on the bus bench, his curly blond hair wild as if he had run to meet her there. Couldn't he take a hint? She had avoided him at school today and even told one of his friends she wasn't interested. Why did so many guys think *no* meant *yes*?

"Well?" the girl with the boa said in a peeved voice.

Serena was standing in their circle.

"Sorry." She inched back.

Jerome turned and waved, his broad smile enticing. "Serena!"

She turned abruptly, pretending not to see him, and ducked into a tight corridor between Tattoo You and a dress shop called Streetwise. She headed toward the alley. She didn't think Jerome would follow her there and chance a run-in with the homeless punkers who claimed the back side of Melrose.

She sighed. Any other girl at La Brea High would have been flattered to have him pursue her. They found his laid-back scruffy look irresistible, even with his bad reputation as a heartbreaker. Serena had caught him staring at her in English class and had wondered what he wanted with her. She wasn't the glam type of girl he normally dated, not with her combat boots, black fishnet hose, and graffiti-painted nails. But it didn't take much to realize he had a huge crush on her. He always seemed to show up where she was.

At first Serena had been impressed that he wasn't the kind of guy who judged a girl by the way she dressed. She might have even dated him if she hadn't discovered the truth. He lied about the girls he had gone out with.

It wasn't as if Serena didn't know guys did that. She knew they exaggerated sometimes, but Jerome did more. She couldn't confront him or even tell others what she knew, though, because no one would believe her.

She had almost reached the alley when her knee-length skirt caught on the jagged edge of a metal trash can. She clicked her tongue ring nervously against her teeth and yanked hard, ripping the material and toppling the can. Papers flew around her.

"Serena."

Frantic, she glanced down the corridor but didn't see anyone. Who had called her name?

Maybe it had only been a trick of the wind gusting through the passageway.

She dodged into the alley and smashed into a frail elderly woman in an orange coat who had been turning the corner.

"Sorry," Serena said, looking around her.

The woman jerked to the side as if she were afraid Serena was going to lunge at her again. This time she did lose her balance. Her wide-brimmed yellow hat sailed to the ground as she fell back, swaying, her gold sandals scraping unsteadily on the asphalt.

Serena dropped her cello case and grabbed the woman's bony arm before she fell.

The woman clung to her, her flowery perfume filling the air between them, but the sweet fragrance didn't cover another, dusty mothball smell. The musty scent rushed into Serena's nose and mouth, making her eyes water, and at once she felt an odd sensation of something drawing breath from her body. She clutched her throat and listened helplessly to the dry whistle of air rushing from her collapsing lungs.

The woman eased her to the ground with a strength that seemed odd coming from her brittle-looking body. She knelt beside Serena, untwisting the cap on a bottled water, then pushed the end between Serena's lips.

"Drink," the woman coaxed, and began pouring.

Water flooded into Serena's mouth, but instead of soothing, it burned, tasting of bitter orange. Serena tried to spit, but the woman clamped her thin cold fingers over Serena's mouth, forcing her to swallow. The liquid seared her throat as a strange heaviness spread through her body, leaving her numb and unable to move. She blinked against the dark clouds pushing into her vision and wondered what the woman had given her.

The woman smiled, and her cold radiant eyes were the last thing Serena remembered.

It was full dark when Serena regained consciousness in the alley. Cold air drifted around her, rustling the newspapers scattered over her. She groaned softly and lay still, waiting for her mind to focus. A faint scent hung in the air, delicate and sweet. At once the memory of what had happened came back to her.

Her hand shot up, pressing against her chest as her lungs pulled in long draws of air. She tasted the lingering bitterness from the water, rolled to her side, and spit. What had the old woman tried to do to her?

Los Angeles was filled with homeless people, but the woman hadn't had the unclean look of someone living under cardboard, and her eyes didn't have the vacant stare of a person who was detached from the world around her.

Serena pulled herself up, feeling faint. A dull pounding began in the back of her head, and she leaned against the brick building until her dizziness passed.

Her stomach grumbled. Her brother, Collin, had warned her that she hadn't been eating or sleeping enough. Maybe low blood sugar and lack of sleep had made her pass out. She wiped her eyes. The only thing she wanted now was to be at home in the kitchen, cramming peanut-butter sandwiches into her mouth. She picked up her cello, heaved the strap of her bag over her shoulder, and started down the corridor toward the sounds of music and traffic coming from Melrose Avenue.

A sense of comfort filled her as she walked on the familiar street, passing coffeehouses and closed boutiques. Three bare-chested punkers huddled near the entrance of a Thai restaurant, their hair jutting in colored spikes, hoops piercing nipples, brows, nose, and lips. She stared at them. They thought they lived on the dark side, but they weren't the ones who made a Los Angeles night dangerous. They watched her, wary expressions on their faces as if they sensed something different about her. When they caught her gaze, they turned and ambled away.

Near the next corner, two cars swerved around a slow-moving Lexus and sped through the intersection. The Lexus pulled to the curb in front of Serena and stopped, motor idling, its black metal reflecting the red neon lights from a nearby store. Tinted windows gave the car a sinister look and made it impossible to see the driver or the passengers inside. Serena wondered briefly if some rock star was trolling Melrose, looking for a date.

She turned and started down a quiet residential street lined with jacaranda trees. She had gone two blocks when headlights appeared behind her, casting white light over the purple flowers falling from the trees. She assumed the driver was searching for an address, but when the car continued rolling slowly behind her, her body tensed.

At the next street she passed around an iron fence, changing her normal path home. The large houses, spaced farther apart here, made the shadows seem deeper. Her footsteps were the only sound she heard at first, and then the soft rumble of a car engine filled the night.

Suddenly headlights glared behind her again, closer than before. She glanced back, certain it was the Lexus.

Her alarm sharpened into fear. She resisted

the urge to run, forcing her pace to remain slow, but when she neared the next corner, she shot at an angle across a wet lawn, crushing through a bed of petunias, purposefully going in the wrong direction, away from her house and back toward Melrose Avenue. She sprinted down the gloomy street, her cello and book bag pounding painfully against her, eyes scanning the shadows for a place to hide.

The car engine revved. At any moment the Lexus would turn the corner, headlights flaring. She vaulted over a small picket fence, tossed her cello case and messenger bag into a bush of overgrown junipers, and dove behind a thick hedge of rosebushes. Thorns snared her sweater, pricking through to her skin. She ducked low and waited, breathing the damp earthly smells.

The car sped around the corner, a hubcap scraping the concrete curb, and stopped with a jerk. The pressure of the engine roared against the restraint of the brakes as if the car were a fierce living machine anxious to be released to pursue its prey.

Serena kept hidden, heart racing, and glanced down at her amulet, studying the face of the moon etched in the metal. The charm had been given to her at birth and was a symbol of her true identity. She sensed that what was happening to her now was somehow connected to her secret.

The car inched forward, taillights painting the white exhaust red, making it impossible to see the license plate.

She wondered if Followers of the Atrox were staring out at the street from behind the tinted glass windows. They were forever trying to trap her, because once the Daughters of the Moon were destroyed, the Atrox could bring about the ruin of humankind. She could use her power to read the driver's intentions, but using her gift right now might be risky. Many Followers had the same ability and would use the mental connection to find her.

With a sudden blast the Lexus took off, but instead of getting up, Serena huddled deeper into the shadows, waiting. When she was certain the car wasn't just circling the block, she stood, brushed the gluey cobwebs from her face and arms, then found her cello and bag and started walking.

She kept close to the houses now, walking in shadows, always conscious of the next place to hide. When she felt safe again, she sprinted down the sidewalk, at last turning onto the tinted stone walkway that led to the large Spanish-style house where she lived with her father and brother.

Normally she loved the balconies and tiled roof, but the night had left her tense and suspicious. Wind ruffled through the palm fronds, brushing spiky shadows across the facade. Even the ceramic frogs and trolls sitting on the redwood chips in the planters seemed to have taken on a threatening appearance.

She unlocked the front door and hurried inside, slamming the door behind her, the sound echoing as she dropped her books and cello case to the floor. She turned and slid the dead bolt in place, then switched on the light.

"Hello?" No one answered her call, but she hadn't expected her father or Collin to be home yet.

A clicking sound made her look down. Wally, her pet raccoon, ran to greet her, his toenails tapping on the tile floor. But when she bent to scoop him into her arms, he backed away, then cocked his head, nostrils testing the air.

"What's the matter, Wally?" she asked in a high, coaxing voice. "Com'ere."

Wally turned, his tail high in the air like a flag, and dashed back into the darkness. That was odd. He had never run from her before. She shrugged and had started to pass the huge gold-framed mirror in the entrance when she caught her reflection. What she saw made her heart lurch. She turned back and studied her face, smoothing her fingers over her brow bones to her temple. She'd had the strangest sensation that someone else had peered back at her from behind her own eyes.

AFTER SERENA HAD eaten and showered, she crawled into bed, the throbbing pain
continuing in the back of her head. She snuggled
under the covers and had started to close her eyes
when she caught a cloudy silhouette slipping
across her balcony. She sat up with a start, throwing her bedcovers aside.

Whatever it had been was gone now.

Still, she stepped barefoot across the room,
the floorboards cool beneath her feet. She hadn't
told Collin the real reason she hadn't been sleeping well. Too frequently she dreamed that Stanton

had entered her room and knelt beside her bed, caressing her arm, kissing her cheek, and sometimes speaking to her about their future together.

Afterward she always awoke, heart aching, and it was difficult to go back to sleep. His dreamworld visits felt too real. She had set a line of alarm clocks on her dresser as a precaution. Followers hated timepieces, anything that reminded them of their eternal bond to evil. A clock couldn't stop Stanton the way a crucifix stopped a vampire, but if he did come into her room, she was certain he would turn the clocks to face the wall. Recently they hadn't been disturbed, and that was the only way she knew that his visits were only dreams.

Now she pushed through the French doors and stepped onto the balcony. The porch light below cast an amber glow across the lawn. She leaned over the dew-covered railing, breathing the sweet fragrance of the red roses on the trellis, and studied the black shadows at the edge of the yard, wondering if Stanton were there.

A feeling of terrible loneliness pulsed

through her. Their love had been forbidden because he was a Follower and she was a Daughter. But she had loved him in spite of everything. Even now she tried not to think of what he must have done to become an Immortal. He had been an Invitus before, taken by the Atrox against his will, and she had sensed his struggle to escape his destiny.

But after the Daughters had freed him from his bondage, he had returned to the Atrox. He was no longer Invitus, but someone who had freely chosen evil. She hated him for that choice.

A breeze blew around her, carrying the damp from the ocean. She winced at the sudden chill and went back inside, locking the balcony doors behind her before settling deep under her covers. She felt drowsy and drifted into an uneasy rest.

Hours later she awoke with a start, thirsty and sweating, not sure what had roused her from her sleep. If it had been another dream about Stanton, she could no longer remember it. The clocks looked undisturbed, their ticking the only sound in the quiet house. She still felt sleepy, but instead of pulling the covers tight around her, she climbed from bed, slipped into a robe, and trundled down the hallway, the carpet soft beneath her feet.

At the top of the stairwell she grabbed the banister and made her way without turning on the light. She pushed through the kitchen door and paused, not sure why she had come downstairs, then rummaged through the refrigerator, taking out a jar of green olives. She gobbled down three, then ate a piece of cheesecake, chasing it with a swallow of apple juice from the bottle. At last she grabbed an ice cube from the freezer and pressed it against the dull pain in the back of her head.

Thin branches scraped around the window over the sink. She stepped to the counter and looked out. The moon was almost full but in its waning phase, hanging in the clear sky. At one time, a night without a moon had made her uneasy, but now she felt a spiritual connection to Hekate, the goddess of the dark—a secret she hadn't even told her closest friend, Jimena. She wanted to become a *mystica*, one initiated into the secret rites of Hekate, because she understood the purpose of the dark now. It was necessary for growth. Instead of being something to fear, it needed to be welcomed as a passing from the old to the new.

Thinking about Hekate was the last thing Serena remembered before she was jolted awake, sunlight glaring into her eyes, the smell of freshly brewed coffee wafting around her. She blinked, surprised to find she was still standing in the kitchen. Could she have fallen asleep standing up? She heard someone behind her and turned sharply.

Collin pulled a carton of milk from the refrigerator, his sun-bleached white hair falling on his black sweater. He smiled at her, his blue eyes fresh and alert. "You're up early. You even made coffee already. Did you have trouble sleeping again?"

"Sorta," she mumbled, rubbing her temples. She couldn't remember starting the coffee, scooping the grounds, filling the coffeepot with water.

Collin looked at her with concern. "What's wrong?"

"I'm fine," she answered.

"You don't look *fine*." He sat at the table and shook Wheat Chex into his bowl.

She had started to pour a cup of coffee when an odd soreness in her hand made her glance down. She saw a slash cut across the tip of her index finger. A small knife lay on the counter in front of her, three drops of blood near the tip. Her eyes continued to the white porcelain sink and with a shock read YOU'RE NOT ALONE ANY-MORE crudely written in blood.

She glanced back at Collin, hoping he hadn't seen the sudden fear on her face.

He was too busy spooning cereal into his mouth and reading a text on Greek mythology.

She turned on the faucet and washed the message away, then stared at the cut on her finger. She had read about sleepwalkers doing bizarre things like eating and talking and even mowing the lawn in the middle of the night. She supposed it was possible to sleep while standing up, then slice her finger and write the message, acting out a dream, but the idea sent a shudder of fear through her. Because lately her dreams had all been nightmares.

CHAPTER THREE

T HE BACK DOOR opened, and Jimena walked through the sunlight cascading into the kitchen. Her jeans were cut tight and sexy low, revealing her hipbones and the old gang tattoos across her stomach. A short-sleeved tee showed off the crescent moon and star on her arm, but the two blue teardrops under her eye were now covered with makeup. She shot a glance at Serena. "Why aren't you ready for school?"

Before Serena could answer, Jimena saw Collin sitting at the table. She leaned over him, wrapping her arms around his neck, and kissed his cheek. Her luxurious black hair fell around him as she read over his shoulder.

"Why are you reading about mythology when you got me?" Jimena teased. Like Serena, Jimena was a Daughter of the Moon.

"I'm trying to find out more about you," Collin answered. He had become obsessed with mythology and ancient history after learning the truth about Serena and Jimena. His obsession almost matched his passion for surfing, but not quite.

Jimena sauntered over to the counter, squinting at the sun, and poured herself a mug of coffee. "What's with you, *chica?*" she said to Serena. "You're still in your pajamas."

"She's not sleeping well," Collin said.

"Bad dreams again?" Jimena asked, studying Serena over the rim of her mug, her black eyes worried. "*¿Qué te pasa?* There's something you're not telling me. Are you all right?"

"Maybe." Serena glanced at the cut on her finger. "I have a headache that won't go away."

"Tension," Collin said, and slammed his book. "I got to go." He grabbed his keys.

Serena was grateful that even though Collin was dating Jimena, he always knew when to give them time alone.

Jimena kissed Collin good-bye, then turned back to Serena. "Tell me what's up while you get ready."

In her bedroom Serena recounted what had happened the day before after she had left school.

"It doesn't sound so weird to me," Jimena said when Serena had finished. "The old woman might have been trying to help you and without thinking gave you some water she had mixed with one of her medicines. Remember my grandmother's friend Helena? She couldn't swallow her pills, so she ground them up and mixed them with her tea. If you ever tasted that brew, you'd swear you were drinking rat poison."

Serena flipped her hair forward, moussing the long ends while her head was upside down. "But what about the Lexus?"

"It could have been Followers, but I don't think they would have given up so easily. Plus you were on the street alone, out late. It was probably some old guy wanting to party with you. That's as dangerous as a carload of Followers."

"And what about the message in the sink?" Serena asked.

"'You're not alone anymore,'" Jimena repeated, considering. "It must have been part of a dream."

Serena shuddered. "It's creepy to think I acted out a dream like that."

"*Mi abuelita* . . . my grandmother tells stories about women who get up in the middle of the night and clean their apartments. In the morning they can't remember doing it because they were sleepwalking."

"I guess that's what I did." Serena rolled red tint over her lips, then started for the hallway. "Let's get out of here."

They hurried down the stairs. At the front door Serena picked up her book bag and cello.

"All that extracurricular stuff can add stress to your life," Jimena said as they walked out to the blue-and-white '81 Oldsmobile waiting in the drive. Jimena's brother let her use the car when he was visiting from San Diego even though she didn't have a driver's license.

"You think stress is making me walk in my sleep?" Serena loaded her cello into the back, then threw her book bag on the floor. With a sudden start she realized she hadn't done her homework. She sighed heavily and climbed into the front seat next to Jimena.

"You're doing too many things at once," Jimena assured her, and turned the key. The mufflers rumbled. She backed the car from the driveway, then dropped the gearshift into drive and headed toward La Brea High.

"A lot of kids do more," Serena said. "Just look at all the things Vanessa is into, and Tianna, too."

"But you're taking classes at UCLA," Jimena pointed out. "Along with your high-school schedule, plus you practice your cello every day and play with the school orchestra, and if that isn't enough, you read tarot cards for every girl with a problem."

"I guess." Serena looked out the window at the houses speeding by.

"When do you ever have time for yourself?" Jimena asked. "You never just kick it like we used to. You're always so busy since . . ." Her words fell away, and she shook her head.

She didn't need to complete the sentence. Serena knew she was talking about her breakup with Stanton. She had kept busy as a way to avoid thinking about him.

"You're right," Serena admitted, her stomach tightening as she thought about what he had done.

"Maybe it's time to find someone else," Jimena suggested.

"Maybe," Serena answered softly.

"It's not as if you don't have anyone who wants to take you out," Jimena encouraged. "They're lined up."

Serena shrugged. "It's just that I can see what's on their minds, and believe me—it can be a big turnoff." She thought of Jerome, wishing she had never gone inside his head.

"Where have you been living?" Jimena asked. "Every girl knows what's on a guy's mind."

"But I get the details." Serena laughed. "Sometimes reading a guy's mind is a curse." Other times it was an embarrassment, like with the first guy she had dated. He had been thinking how much he liked her and she had answered his thoughts out loud, carrying on a conversation with him. It was only when she saw the amazed look on his face that she realized he hadn't uttered a word. She still felt embarrassed when she saw him at school, but fortunately he avoided her.

"Just stop picking up their thoughts," Jimena said, as if it were easy to do. "The mystery is half the fun of dating."

"Yeah," Serena agreed. "It's just that sometimes I sense something, and then I can't resist going into the guy's mind and checking it out."

"But you always wish you hadn't, after," Jimena reminded her.

"I know."

"Maybe things are about to change." Jimena couldn't stop grinning.

"What?" Serena asked.

"I had a premonition of you at the foam

party, with some guy like you couldn't get enough of him. You were all over him, kissing and dancing." The ability to see the future was Jimena's gift.

"You saw me kissing a guy?" Serena looked shocked. "Who?"

"I didn't see his face," Jimena admitted. "And it wasn't exactly a premonition, either. I was using this new part of my power."

"So it worked?" Serena felt excitement rising inside her. Maggie was their mentor and guide. Before she had left for Santorini, she had been teaching Jimena how to expand her gift to see the future without having to wait for a premonition to hit her.

"Not exactly," Jimena confessed. "I'm not having too much success with it so far, but I did see you with your arms around some guy. Soap bubbles were dripping all over you."

"Next time peek at his face." Serena smiled, her mood finally lifting.

"I'll keep working at it," Jimena promised. "But most of the time I just get this jumble of pictures that makes no sense."

Serena nodded.

"Maggie warned me that my imagination would play tricks on me." Jimena turned the car into the student parking lot, her eyes searching for a parking space. "Like last night when I tried to work it and see *el futuro*, I saw you and Stanton united against Followers who wanted to overthrow the Atrox. Can you imagine that?"

Serena shook her head, sad thoughts returning. "That will never happen. I'll never be able to forgive him."

CHAPTER FOUR

AT THE END OF the day Serena sat on the sprawling lawn at the back of the school, waiting for her friends. She tore the elastic from her ponytail and rushed her fingers through her hair, wishing the pain would go away. Another time she might have canceled, but she had been waiting months for the psychic bazaar. Catty's mother had asked them to come early. It was the first time she was going to tell fortunes by reading coffee grounds, and she was concerned no one would come to her booth.

On the field in front of her the boys' soccer

team ran in groups of three, kicking the ball back and forth between them in a drill. Jerome was the team captain. He caught the ball against his chest and, leaning back, bounced it up and down on his knee before letting it fall. He swirled around, hitting the ball with a back-heel pass, and sent it to the next player. His teammates whooped and applauded. He glanced at Serena, his blond curls clinging to the sweat on his forehead. She hoped he didn't think she had come here to watch him.

"Hey." Tianna was the first to arrive, her excitement obvious. "Do you think Catty's mom can really see the future in a coffee cup?" She wore a thermal T-shirt and a track jacket. Her long, silky black hair was braided, loose tendrils falling into her eyes.

"I guess we'll find out." Serena smiled.

Tianna was the one who most resembled a goddess even though she wasn't born a Daughter. She had become one after using her telekinetic powers to save the others.

"There's Catty." Tianna sat in the grass next to Serena.

Catty ran across the field, dodging guys kicking soccer balls around an obstacle course of orange cones. Her denim trench coat flapped around her, revealing a short tee and Levi's low riders; a jewel hung over her navel from a peekaboo pierce.

"You've been time traveling," Serena said when Catty stood in front of them.

"How'd you know?" Catty pushed her brown hair behind her ears. She had a sunshine smile.

"There's way too much sizzle in that outfit." Tianna laughed. "You'd have definitely been sent home if you'd worn that to class. Besides, I didn't see you all day."

"You missed me?" Catty asked, breathless. "I was just checking out the foam party. It's going to be so much fun."

That was Catty's gift. She could time travel in short spurts. When she tried longer jumps, she got stuck in the tunnel, the hole in time she used to go from one time to the next.

"That's not fair," Tianna complained playfully. "You get to go to the party before it even happens."

"So do I have a good time?" Serena asked, remembering what Jimena had told her earlier.

"Do you ever have a bad time?" Catty smirked and started walking. "Come on. Jimena wants us to meet her at the car."

They hurried out to the parking lot.

Vanessa was already there, leaning against the trunk of the car, her red sleeveless turtleneck pulled up, exposing her tan midriff, her legs stretching out from a short black skirt, catching the sun. Her blond hair, held back by black barrettes, fell in long, sinuous curls around her.

Catty jumped next to Vanessa, startling her out of her reverie.

She jerked up, lifting her shades, eyes searching for danger. "Don't scare me like that," she warned, and glanced down at her hands. Like the others, Vanessa had a special ability. She could become invisible. But intense emotions, like fear, made her lose control of her power.

She shook out her hands now, as if she were trying to press her molecules back together. Invisibility was a big problem for her. When she had first started dating Michael Saratoga, she had begun to disappear every time he tried to kiss her.

Jimena ran over to them, jiggling the car keys. "Ready?" She pulled off the bulky sweater she'd worn at school to cover her bare stomach.

"Mom is going to be so happy that we're all going to show up." Catty opened the rear car door.

"It should be fun." Serena slid into the front.

When they were all in and buckled up, Jimena turned the key in the ignition, pressed her foot on the accelerator, and revved the engine before steering through the parking lot, taking careful turns around the kids gathered in small groups there.

Soon they were heading down Santa Monica Boulevard toward the beach. Jimena switched on the music, adjusting the volume until the beat made the dashboard tremble. They sang along with the radio.

Novelty shops, boutiques, souvenir shops, coffeehouses, movie theaters, and bookstores blurred past them. By the time the car tunneled under the San Diego Freeway, everyone had stopped singing to listen to Vanessa, her voice unrestrained and soul-stirring. She sang with Michael's band now and even wrote her own songs.

Finally they parked and walked through the street performers crowding near the hall entrance. Catty handed their free passes to a lady in a red-and-gold sari standing at the door, and then they went inside the huge auditorium. They ambled through the crowd, the scents of lavender, peppermint, and rosemary drifting around them from the aromatherapy booth. The PA system piped in mellow New Age music, but the dreamy sounds could barely be heard over the excited chatter of the people inside. A long line was already forming in front of the palm reader.

"Mom's in stall twenty-nine," Catty said, and started around another booth.

Tianna stopped and stared at a woman doing past-life regression. "Do you think that's real?"

Serena nodded. "I've tried it. It feels like a

trance, and you really do see yourself in another time."

"Vanessa kept going in and out of focus when she did it," Catty teased. "We had to pull her away."

"It was scary," Vanessa said defensively, and started to move on.

Dr. Wen did Chinese face reading at the next stall. He sat at a table, staring at a woman with a long slim face and large ears. Her skin was deeply wrinkled, as if she had withstood harsh weather. The doctor studied her, writing notes on a yellow pad where he had sketched an outline of her head.

"Let's try this after," Tianna said excitedly.

"There's Kendra." Jimena pointed.

Serena turned and started following Catty and Jimena through the people straining to watch the face divination.

Kendra stood under a sign saying THE FUTURE IN A CUP OF COFFEE. She waved when she saw them, her narrow face breaking into a huge smile. Purple ribbons were threaded through the braids on top of her head, dangling down to the nape of her loose-fitting lavender dress. It didn't look as if she'd had any customers yet. The white tablecloth looked too fresh, and no used cups sat in the gray plastic tubs waiting for dirty dishes.

The aroma of coffee became stronger as they neared her booth.

"I'm so glad you came." She hugged each of them, then settled behind a table set up with an electric burner. Cups and saucers were stacked in a cardboard box behind her next to bags of ground coffee and sugar.

They grabbed chairs and scooted closer.

"Coffee must be prepared with care for the reading to be a good one," she explained, wrapping her fingers around the long handle of a small pan and swirling it over the red-hot coils of the burner. "This pan is called a *cezve*. The old fortune-tellers used to roast, grind, and brew their own coffee."

She removed the pan from the burner and poured the froth into five white porcelain cups set in front of them. She handed Serena a cup with the handle pointing toward her. "Use both hands to hold the cup and concentrate on something important in your life."

Serena lifted her cup, savoring the strong aroma before sipping, then the sweet rich flavor filled her mouth. She didn't want to think about Stanton, and tried instead to focus on her music. But pictures of him kept intruding. She glanced at the others. They drank their coffee, each staring out, lost in their own thoughts.

When they had emptied their cups, Kendra spoke again. "Swirl the grounds around and turn your cup upside down on the saucer." She waited until they had. "Now we wait for the grounds to cool and settle."

When the cups had cooled, Kendra turned Vanessa's over and examined her grounds, then glanced at the ones still on the saucer. "This one is easy," Kendra said. "See the fish? That means good fortune, especially on the rim. Blessings are swimming your way."

Vanessa smiled.

"Dip your finger in the grounds, then suck

them off your finger to seal your fate," Kendra told her.

Vanessa did, and Kendra looked inside Jimena's cup.

"Birds." Kendra laughed. "Of course, there would be lots of birds for Jimena, because she receives omens. You see the future clearly, but sometimes you don't believe in the power you have."

Jimena leaned forward. "I see the birds. *Pájaros* flying all over the cup."

Next Kendra glanced at Catty, then studied the brown zigzag design inside her cup. "A road." She sighed. "Travel, of course, and specifically time traveling. The road moves back and forth over the bottom of the cup, which represents the past, and up to the top, which stands for the future. Catty will be taking innumerable trips."

"Try mine," Tianna asked, nudging hers forward.

Kendra turned it over, her smile fading. "A heavy heart." She pointed to the lump stuck in the bottom of Tianna's cup. "You're still recovering from a loss in the past." She didn't need to say more. Followers had killed Tianna's parents and her sister. It was only since she had been living in a stable foster home that she had begun to grieve.

"Last one," Kendra said, turning Serena's cup.

Serena leaned forward. It looked like snakes coiled around the top of her cup.

Kendra set the cup down with a loud clatter and placed the saucer on top of it.

"What did you see?" Serena asked.

"Sometimes I make mistakes," Kendra said quickly.

"I'm sure you didn't," Serena coaxed. "Tell me anyway."

"I'll do a reading for you another time." Kendra tried to smile, but her lips quivered.

Serena knew she was trying to hide something from her. She twisted into Kendra's mind, but what she read baffled her. *An enemy has come to visit.* Why would Kendra be upset over that? Followers were always trying to hunt them down. But when she glanced at Kendra's face, she knew there was something more Kendra was trying to keep from her. What had she seen that she didn't want to say?

Before Serena could probe deeper, Catty interrupted her. "There's Morgan."

Serena pulled from Kendra's mind and followed Catty's pointing finger to a booth up the aisle.

Morgan held a purple charm up to the display light, her blond hair shimmering. She looked as confident as always but with more attitude now. She wore a black leather jacket, lacy pink camisole, and stiletto ankle boots. Guys always got a dreamy look when Morgan was around. She'd had a big crush on Collin once.

"We better go check her out," Serena said, and stood to leave, grateful to see a line forming for Kendra's booth.

Kendra mouthed a thank-you as they walked away.

"Who's Morgan?" Tianna asked.

"She used to be an Initiate," Vanessa explained. "She got involved with a Follower named Cassandra, because she wanted to prove herself worthy of joining up with the Atrox."

"But Cassandra's scheme failed," Serena added.

"Her parents thought Morgan was delusional," Vanessa went on. "So they placed her in one of those pricey hospitals in the valley for troubled teens."

"When did she get released?" Catty asked.

"I don't know." Vanessa shrugged.

"Let's see what she's up to." Jimena edged up to the booth.

Morgan held a blue amulet and raised a perfectly arched brow. A gold hoop pierced the flesh above her eye. "Are you sure this one will protect me from evil?"

There was an urgency in her voice that made the vendor stare at her before nodding. "That one will protect you against evil."

Morgan smiled. "Good." She laid a twenty-dollar bill on the table, ignored the vendor's offer of a bag, and slipped the leather thong around her neck.

"Hey, Morgan." Serena eased next to her.

Jimena grabbed her arm on the other side.

Morgan turned to leave, but Vanessa, Catty, and Tianna had formed a barricade behind her.

"Can't you guys leave me alone?" Her voice was arrogant, but there was also fear in it.

"Why are you buying a charm against evil?" Jimena asked.

"After what I've been through, wouldn't you?" Morgan sneered.

"But there must be a reason you waited until now," Tianna said.

"I suppose," Morgan answered.

"What do you know that you're not saying?" Vanessa spoke softly. "Maybe we can help you."

Serena didn't wait to hear her answer but pressed into her mind. Intense fear had snarled Morgan's thoughts, and the fierce emotion made it difficult to draw out a single idea or memory. Suddenly Serena felt Morgan pull back as if she had been hit. Serena broke from her thoughts, startled. She was positive Morgan wasn't strong enough to have sensed her invasion.

Morgan stared at her with disdain. "I can't believe you don't know what's happening, but as long as you don't, you're definitely not going to find out about it from me. I want out of all this. I don't want to be on your side or theirs."

Jimena moved aside, and Morgan squeezed around her.

"What's with her?" Catty had a puzzled look on her face.

"She's hiding something big," Serena said. "And she's scared."

"Yeah, but of what?" Jimena asked.

CHAPTER FIVE

WEDNESDAY AFTERNOON, Serena stood in front of her locker, feeling dazed and unable to remember what she had done over the past three hours. She had a fuzzy memory of eating a hot dog at Pink's with Jimena, but the rest of the time seemed lost to her. She glanced down at the unfamiliar doodles curling around the edge of her spiral notebook and felt a vague recollection of her hand absently drawing while she listened to the substitute teacher in history class, but the foggy picture seemed like a faraway childhood memory. Could she have become that sleepy and dozed off in all her classes?

She was definitely going to cut back her

schedule. The strange muddled feeling inside her head scared her.

"Hey." Jimena came up beside her. "You want me to wait around and give you a ride home?"

"Wait around for what?" Serena asked before remembering that she had orchestra practice this afternoon. She fished her house keys from her bag and tossed them to Jimena. "I'll take the bus. Can you feed Wally for me?"

Jimena caught the keys. "Sure. Anything else?"

"No." Serena opened her locker. "I'll meet you later at my house."

"See you then." Jimena hurried away, disappearing in the crush of students.

Serena tossed her notebook into the locker. It landed on a haphazard pile of books. If she had any homework assignments, she couldn't remember them now. She slammed the metal door, then turned sharply, bumping into Jerome.

"Hey, Serena." He stared at her in a sensual way, his smile eager and warm. He seemed so self-assured. If she hadn't known his inner thoughts, she could have easily fallen for him.

Three freshmen girls walked by, their books clutched tight against their chests. "Hi, Jerome!" they called in high-pitched unison before they broke into giggles.

He waved and started talking to them.

Serena used the distraction to twist inside his mind and trace through his network of memories until she found the one of his seeing her Monday afternoon on Melrose Avenue. She watched in fascination as his memory played for her as if it were her own. He had chased after her down the narrow corridor, but when he had come to the alley, he hadn't seen her. A strange wind had swept around him, frightening him. That surprised her. What was it?

Then she studied the details in slow motion, looking at the newspapers fluttering against the brick wall and wondering if she had been lying beneath the flapping pages. Serena saw nothing of the old woman, but it seemed doubtful that she could have gotten away so quickly. Perhaps she had hidden when she heard Jerome coming.

"Serena?" Jerome called her name.

She pulled from his mind, blinking.

"You were staring at me funny," he said.

"Sorry. I've been distracted lately. I've got orchestra practice." She started heading toward the school auditorium.

"I'll go with you." Jerome shoved through the jostling crowd, trying to keep up with her. "I'm glad I finally have a chance to talk to you."

"I don't have time right now," she said, quickening her pace.

"Wait." He grabbed her arm, pulling her over to the lockers away from the stream of kids pushing down the hallway. "I've been wanting to talk to you since you read your poem in English class."

"Which one?" She had read maybe fourteen poems over the semester.

"The one about your demon lover." Something in his eyes gleamed as if he knew her secret.

An involuntary blush rose to her cheeks. She wished she hadn't read that poem about Stanton. It had laid open her heart, exposing feelings she hadn't meant to share.

"I really identified with the guy not knowing

his own soul," he said, suddenly becoming self-conscious.

"You did?" she asked, remembering the webbing of lies that laced around his memories. She wondered if he was telling the truth now. He looked sincere.

"Yeah." He pulled a piece of notebook paper from his back pocket and unfolded it. He had opened and closed it so many times that the page was beginning to tear along the fold lines.

"Where did you find that?" she asked, recognizing her writing.

"You tossed it in the trash." He glanced up at her, his face earnest. "I hope you don't mind. I waited until everyone had left the classroom and then I fished it out."

"I'm just surprised." She remembered throwing it away. "The poem meant that much to you?"

"It touched something inside me," he went on. "I mean, I can't figure it out exactly, but I felt like it was about me."

"The emotion is the important part," she answered, wondering why he would think it was about him. "If it has special meaning to you, then it worked. Thanks." She turned and started to walk away.

He caught up with her. "But you didn't answer my question."

She looked at him, baffled.

"Did you write it for me?" There was too much hope in his eyes.

She started to shake her head and stopped. She hadn't sensed anything evil about him when she'd been in his mind, so how could he identify with what she'd written? She stared at him, wondering if he had suffered like Stanton, trying to control his behavior, hoping that if he could resist long enough, he would have power over it.

"Well?" he asked impatiently.

"It's no one I know," she lied. "Besides, I don't see you as that kind of person, Jerome."

He held up the paper as if he wanted her to read what she had written. "But you loved him in spite of everything he'd done," Jerome reminded her.

"It's just a poem." She hurried away from

him, threading through the kids leaving school.

This time he didn't follow her, but she could feel his thoughts, cutting through the air behind her. She was a challenge to him, and he wasn't going to stop chasing her until he had caught her. His promise felt like a threat. She glanced back at him. He was standing in the middle of the crowded hall, staring at her, his eyes flinty and filled with an anger she hadn't seen there before. It made her uneasy.

She turned the corner and sprinted down a side corridor. She had only gone a short distance when a sense of impending doom came over her. The noise around her became a clash of air-ripping, indistinct sounds. She stopped, her trembling fingers twisting into her hair, bewildered by what she felt. She couldn't breathe, and she sensed danger, but from what? She swirled around, looking at the familiar faces of the kids pushing by her. Some smiled. Others waved. No one seemed dangerous. She didn't understand the need to flee, but instinct told her to run. She dashed crazily, her arms pumping at her sides.

Near the auditorium someone grabbed her arm. She let out a startled cry.

"Serena, are you all right?" A guy named Kyle held her. He wore long earrings and silver chains fashioned from skulls. His eyes were hidden behind dark shades.

"Yeah, why?" Serena asked, hating the breathless tremor in her voice.

"You sure?" he asked.

She felt suddenly dizzy and wished she could catch her breath, but more than anything she needed to get away.

"You don't look okay." He lifted his shades to the top of his head and studied her eyes. "Did someone give you something? You look like you're having a bad trip."

"I'm fine." But her words seemed lost in panic, and she couldn't make her mind focus. She rubbed her hands over her face. Her skin felt clammy and cold.

"Let me get someone to give you a ride home," he offered.

She shook her head, dreading the claustrophobic

feeling of being locked inside a car. "I have practice this afternoon." But already she knew she wasn't going to go. She couldn't sit still in the hollow auditorium and concentrate on music.

The need to escape became suddenly intolerable. She shoved around him, knocking into kids, and hurried to the bus stop, glancing constantly over her shoulder.

She squeezed onto the bus bench, forcing three women to move closer together. Her heart hammered loudly in her ears, nerves stretched to the breaking point—and then she knew. Someone was watching her. She looked up.

A black Lexus with tinted windows was parked across the street. Zillions of luxury cars drove on the streets in Los Angeles, and many celebrities tinted their glass for privacy, so the car's appearance could have been just a bizarre coincidence. Still, her eyes followed it as it merged into traffic. The designer plate read STAR. That was an easy one to remember.

CHAPTER SIX

"YOU DON'T UNDERSTAND." Serena sat on the redwood picnic table in the backyard, talking to Jimena. "It wasn't a Follower doing something to me. There was something wrong inside me." She stared up at the tree branches rustling lazily in the late afternoon breeze, feeling dumbfounded. The terrible fear was gone now, leaving only exhaustion in its place.

"I think you had a panic attack," Jimena said softly, pouring clear golden brown liquid from a pitcher into a glass. She handed it to Serena. "This will help. It's *juego de tamarindo*."

Collin pulled drove his utility van into the

drive, beeped the horn twice, and paused for the automatic garage door to open.

Jimena waved.

Serena sipped the tart, sweet juice, then finished telling Jimena about the odd sensations she had felt earlier.

Soon Collin was walking across the lawn toward them, wearing khaki pants and a white T-shirt, a black sweater tied around his waist.

"I'm all right now." Serena set down the empty glass. "But I need to go back to school and get my cello so I can practice."

"Maybe you should go to bed early and not worry about it," Jimena suggested.

Collin set his books on the table. "Worry about what?" He glanced at Serena, and his smiled faded into a look of concern.

"Serena's not feeling well," Jimena answered.

Collin didn't appear to have heard her. He was staring at her strangely, hands resting on his books, eyes anxious as if he were debating whether or not he should take Serena over to emergency at Cedars-Sinai Hospital.

Serena shuddered, remembering the haunted reflection she had seen in the mirror Monday night. She wondered if Collin and Jimena were seeing that same odd glint in her eyes now.

Two hours later Serena awakened from a nap, feeling better except for a dull throb in the back of her head. She left her bedroom and walked down to the kitchen. Jimena was sitting at the table with Collin, helping him with his mythology.

"I don't care what the book says," Jimena argued. "*No es así.* That's just not the way it is."

Collin smiled. "But I have to learn it like the teacher says. If I mention the Atrox, he'll think I'm nuts."

"Okay," Jimena relented, and rested her hand on his arm. "Repeat the story the way the book's got it."

"Thanks." Collin laughed and traced his hand over her cheek, then pulled her to him for a kiss before returning to his notebook.

Serena stayed at the door, watching them. Jimena had disliked Collin when she first met him, and Serena had hated their constant bickering. But now she felt jealous of what they had. An unexpected longing rose inside her. She wished she could meet someone.

A sudden idea flickered across her mind. If she was so envious of what Collin and Jimena had together, then why didn't she contact Stanton? *Stanton?* She was certain someone else had put the notion into her head, but who?

She stared at Collin and Jimena. She couldn't be picking up their thoughts; they weren't even aware of her presence. Besides, they were too engrossed in each other, heads inches apart, reading Collin's notes.

She rushed to the other side of the kitchen, accidentally kicking Wally's food dish. It clattered across the linoleum.

Jimena looked up, startled, and pushed back her chair with a loud scrape. "What's the matter?"

Serena didn't answer but continued to the open window, concentrating on the view outside, searching for any movement that might betray a Follower.

Collin stepped beside her, resting a hand on her shoulder. "Are you having another panic attack?"

"No," she answered brusquely, pulling away from him. She darted through the utility porch, her bare feet slapping the floor, then opened the back door and ran to the edge of the lawn, her body on fire, ready to face the challenge. She whirled around, scanning the shadows.

"Show yourself," she demanded in a whisper.

Some of the Followers, like Stanton, were shape changers who glided through the night unseen. Stanton had been able to dissolve into shadow and stay that way for days if he wanted. It was one of the skills granted to him by the Atrox. Now she imagined he had even greater powers.

The velvet blackness pressed around her, heavy with promise. An enemy was nearby, but where? She pushed out with her mind, hunting for a flicker of thought that didn't belong. She caught the dream of a neighbor, the stealthy silence of a teenager sneaking from her bedroom window, and the steady stream of words from someone reading a book, but nothing that shouldn't be there.

Still, she discerned another presence. She rubbed the tips of her fingers against her temples, concentrating.

The wind changed abruptly and a sudden shadow spiraled around her, making her body prickle.

"Stanton?" she whispered, her power surging through her, ready to attack. Had he come back with a plan to destroy her? Her heart filled with surprising heaviness. In his dark world, anything was possible.

She gazed at the gloom near the garage, wondering how many vulnerable girls he had recruited and made into Followers since he had stopped seeing her. The compulsion to steal their hope had pulsed through him like a fierce need. It was the only way he could forget his own emptiness, yet she was certain she had sometimes filled that void, making him almost human again. That could never happen now.

A breeze rushed through the trees with a haunted sound, twisting shadows back and forth across the lawn. She tried not to think about Stanton, but she couldn't help it. Without a doubt she knew now that someone else was manipulating her mind, but who?

Jimena and Collin stood under the dim amber glow from the porch light, their bodies tense, heads slowly looking around. Neither had any reason to force a thought into her mind. Collin didn't have that kind of power anyway, and Jimena didn't play games.

Serena stood in the cold, spellbound, unable to stop remembering the good times with Stanton. She had a strong memory of the sensual way he had seeped into her mind and brought her back into his, their thoughts melding. She had seen and felt his struggle, known the sweet pain that came over him with the uncontrollable urge to turn someone to the Atrox. He had tried to hide the dark impulse from her, but in the end he had been unable to conceal what he really was, a creature of night and shadow. She had loved him anyway. She hadn't cared what his past had been; she had only been interested in the way he had been with her, his kind and gentle devotion. But now that was gone.

Suddenly Jimena was beside her. "What's going on?"

"Stanton," Serena whispered. "Or some Follower is making me relive memories of him."

"Why?" Jimena stepped closer to her, her eyes huge and alarmed.

"Whoever it is wants me to see him again," Serena answered.

"Some new plot?" Jimena asked, and Serena could feel the energy building inside her. It was coming off her in waves. "You think Stanton's nearby?"

"I don't know," she answered softly.

Collin cut across the lawn and joined them. "Are you sure it's not another—"

"It's not a panic attack," Jimena snapped, as if she now sensed the odd presence also.

"But there's no light coming from your moon stones," Collin pointed out.

Serena glanced down. Her amulet always glowed in warning when Followers were nearby, but now the silver charm lay cold against her chest. Jimena's wasn't shining either.

"Someone's pulling memories into my mind," Serena insisted.

"Maybe you're just remembering," Collin suggested.

"I know I'm right," Serena argued. "And only a Follower has that power."

Even in the gloomy light she could read the disbelief on Collin's face.

She sighed heavily. "The feeling's gone now anyway. Let's go inside." But as she started to turn, she caught a tremor of a thought, as if someone had been trying to hide their presence from her.

"The alley." She swirled around and ran to the gate, lifted the latch, and then, pushing out, ran into the middle of the alley, her bare feet crunching down on gravel. She looked both ways.

A car sped toward her, headlights glaring.

Jimena and Collin yanked her back. They tumbled into a line of plastic trash cans as the black Lexus whizzed by, its wheels spraying small rocks over them.

Serena turned and caught the license plate STAR. "That's the car that has been following me."

Jimena stood beside her, arms folded over her chest. "Maybe there's a new breed of Follower in town."

CHAPTER SEVEN

TWO DAYS LATER Serena sat on the edge of her bed, painting her toenails a blackish red. Dr. Frank had given her a clean bill of health the day before, saying that her symptoms sounded like hypoglycemia, and had scheduled blood tests for the following week. For now she was to ease up on coffee and sweets. Since then she hadn't had one panic attack or feeling of uneasiness.

She was excited about the foam party tonight but still wasn't sure what to wear. She stared into her closet, feeling a tinge of dissatisfaction with what she saw hanging there. Catty had told her to wear something she didn't mind getting wet and ruined, because the foam quickly turned back to soap and water.

At last she pulled out her Levi's low riders, a thick leather belt, and a new butterfly halter. She had planned to wear the bib halter over a slinky long-sleeve tee, because it was so revealing with its bare back and midriff, but now she shrugged and held it up against her. Why not flaunt it? She was in a partying mood.

She slipped into the jeans and belt, then struggled with the ties on the halter, finally turning to the mirror. Excitement ran through her. She loved the thick leather draped over her hip sand the iridescent blue butterfly wings across her chest. Her hair fell across her shoulders with a luxurious feel. She fluffed the curls, her eyes scintillating with an unfamiliar spark.

Everything about her looked—"Sleek," she whispered out loud, and paused. Where had that word come from? She smiled. Maybe she had picked it up from Catty's mom.

A horn honked outside. She grabbed her

sandals, slipped into them, stuffed her money in a pocket, and hurried to the front door.

Jimena stood beside her car in superlow jeans and a short, silky red shirt with peekaboo cuts down the front. Collin was surfing and was going to meet them later.

"You look ravishing," Serena called from the porch, and started down the walk toward the street.

"I look what?" Jimena paused near the front of the car, one eyebrow raised.

Serena tossed back her head with a short laugh that didn't sound like her own and jumped into the car. "I'm so ready to ride."

"I guess you're feeling better." Jimena shrugged and climbed in behind the steering wheel.

Serena felt an electrifying thrill run through her. "I have so much pizzazz tonight."

"So much *what?*" Jimena asked, her hand stopping in midair, the key pointed at the starter.

Serena thought. That was the third time she'd used an unfamiliar word tonight. "I don't know," she answered finally. "I guess I'm just so happy to be feeling normal again that I'm saying stupid things."

"Glad to have you back." Jimena smiled and turned the key, then jammed the engine, backing the car from the drive with a squeal of brakes.

Half an hour later Jimena parked the car on Vermont Avenue. Planet Bang had rented a building near Wilshire Boulevard for the party. They couldn't use the club in Hollywood because soapsuds would have ruined the hardwood floors and plaster walls.

Serena and Jimena followed the handwritten posters taped to parking meters and streetlight poles. Arrows beneath the signs PLANET BANG PARTY pointed the way. They walked past bargain stores and eateries with advertisements in Korean, Spanish, and English, the spicy smells of Korean barbecue drifting around them.

Security guards in yellow parkas stood inside a recessed entrance under the glare of bare lightbulbs. Curling tan phone wires dangled from their ears, connecting them to security inside.

Kids were lined up against the building,

anxious to party, some already dancing to the music coming from inside. Many held towels rolled around bathing suits.

A sultry smile crossed Jimena's lips as they walked to the end of the line. "Look at all the guys checking us out." She still liked to tease even though Collin remained her one and only.

The line moved quickly and soon they were inside, standing at the edge of the crowded dance floor. The DJ was on a stage in the back, working the turntables, touching his headphones from time to time. Light designs of blue and white jabbed the smoky air, followed by flares of purple and eye-shattering bursts like lightning strikes.

Serena swayed with the beat, scanning the room, breathing the clean detergent scent.

At the edge of the dance floor nonslip stickers like those used in bathtubs made a path across the cement to a large sign that read WET PARTY AREA, dangling from ropes. Behind it, huge sections of white plastic sheeting hung from the ceiling, billowing in and out. A security guard in shorts stood near the flap entrance, making kids slow down and walk. Old pieces of carpeting were scattered around to keep kids from skidding and falling once the foam started to melt. The droning suds machine whined beneath the music and laughter.

Another area was marked off with a sign, CHANGING AREA AND REST ROOMS. Already workers were laying scraps of carpeting over a path of water leading from the foam to the rest rooms.

"Let's go over to the stage first," Jimena said, and started pushing through the dancers. "Everyone's going to meet there."

Vanessa walked across the stage in a lacy corset top and black taffeta slacks with slits up the sides. She was busy setting up amplifiers.

"Serena! Jimena!" Tianna saw them and waved them over, her long boyish bangs accenting her eyes. She wore a tight pink tank top and jeans.

Derek had given Tianna and Catty a ride over. He was Tianna's boyfriend, and the only one at La Brea High who knew their secret. He nodded a greeting. A bandanna tied tight around his head held back his long red hair. His deep blue eyes glanced at Serena, then away. She liked his look, the scattering of freckles across his long even nose.

He held Tianna against him, his arms circling her. She tilted her head, stealing kisses from him.

"Let's go check out the suds," Derek whispered against her ear.

"You try it." Tianna smiled at him. "I'm changing before I go in."

Serena rolled her eyes. She could only imagine how drop-dead gorgeous Tianna must look in a swimsuit.

"See ya," Derek yelled, and disappeared into the dancers, threading his way toward the plastic walls.

"Did you bring something to change into?" Catty asked, spreading lip gloss over her lower lip with her little finger. She had painted flames up the flared bell-bottoms of her hip-hugging jeans, repeating the fiery design around her navel. She wore a tight orange tank, her hair cropped and layered, framing her face.

Before Serena could answer, a hand touched her back. She turned quickly. Jerome stood behind her.

"Want to dance?" He pulled her out to the dance floor, his hands around the bare skin above her waist. "You look great tonight."

She could feel the jealous stares from a few girls dancing nearby.

Jerome was aware of them, too, his eyes flirting even as he spoke to Serena. "I like this DJ. He puts on a good show."

Serena tried to pull away. "I didn't finish talking to my friends."

He acted as if he hadn't heard her, his fingers wandering up her back, urging her closer. She wished she hadn't worn such a revealing top now.

"I like you a lot, Serena," he said against her cheek, his grasp tightening. "And I think you'd like me if you'd just let your feelings go."

"Jerome." She spoke in a warning tone and tried to pry his fingers free.

He looked down at her with a sly smile as if he were enjoying her struggle.

Exasperated, she bulldozed into his mind, scrambling his thoughts.

His hands fell to his sides and he tottered back, colliding into the couple behind him before stumbling and pitching to the side, his eyes glazed like a zombie's.

Serena darted toward the plastic sheeting, knowing his thoughts would come back in a second.

She kicked her sandals into the long pile of shoes and socks. The security guard lifted the flap, and she stepped into four feet of soap foam. Heavy-gauge plastic covered the floor inside, and kids danced in the suds. Overhead, fluorescent lights shined brightly, reflecting off the steady stream of white froth churning from a huge tube hanging from the ceiling. Kids ducked in and out of the bubbling mounds, dancing wildly.

Serena felt someone staring at her and turned. Derek stood in a pile of lather, chest bare, his adorable blue eyes skimming over her body. He blushed when he saw her looking at him. But it wasn't as if Serena hadn't caught his stares a few times before Tianna came into his life. She tilted her head as a shameless craving awakened inside her. She wondered what it would feel like to kiss Derek. Why wonder? She could tell when a guy liked her. She pushed through the foam, picking up a whiff of it in her hand and throwing it at him.

"Hey, Derek." She posed in front of him, stretching her body, lifting her hands around her neck, then combing her fingers through her hair, loving the way he couldn't resist looking at her.

She let his eyes linger, enjoying the thrill of being the huntress. "Want to dance?"

"No," he said nervously, shaking his head, but he obviously meant yes.

"I can read your mind, remember?" she said with a laugh, and grabbed his hand, delighting in the confusion on his face.

"I'm looking for Tianna," he said.

"Liar," she whispered, and eased into the front of his mind, savoring his desire. It made her bolder, and she pressed against him.

"I really like Tianna," he said, then cleared his throat. "We get along great."

She ignored his protests. "You like the way I look tonight, don't you?" She didn't pose it as a question. She knew. His mind was in turmoil, trying to find a way to escape her before he gave in to his body and wrapped his arms around her.

He looked at her cautiously. "You look great, Serena. You always do, but Tianna—"

She placed a foam-covered finger over his lips, sealing his silence. "We're just dancing," she reminded him, and let an insolent smile slide across her face.

She squirmed into his mind and with one ruthless shove pushed all his thoughts about Tianna back with forgotten memories as she summoned up the past, bringing forward the days when he still had a crush on Serena.

He stared at her, eyes wide in wonder as if he were aware of what she was doing, then he relaxed, his wet hands reaching around her waist. She closed her eyes and let her arms wrap around his neck, enjoying his touch. His lips moved across her cheek, soft and hesitating, making her hungry for more, and then he kissed her.

But it didn't have the same feel as Stanton's kiss. Sudden sadness washed over her, then panic rocked her. What had she just done? She liked Derek, but only as a friend.

"Sorry." She dropped her hold on his mind.

His memories crashed back into place. His eyes burst open, looking at her as if she had hit him, his blush almost as red as his hair.

With a jolt she realized that beneath the foam, their bodies were still pressed together. She jumped back and slipped, colliding with someone.

She turned. Tianna stood behind her, looking stunning in her bikini, gold chains draped around her waist.

"That's a strange style of dancing," Tianna said with a sly smile. "Can I cut in?"

"Sure." Serena stared at her, feeling overwhelmed. How was she going to explain the kiss to Tianna when she didn't even comprehend it herself? She shook her head, feeling as if she had been in a trance. "I'm sorry," she muttered again.

Jimena pushed through the soapsuds, joining them. "Foam parties make everyone feel too sexy." She laughed and pulled Serena away.

"I guess so," Tianna agreed, and took Derek's hand.

"Lucky for you Tianna isn't the jealous type," Jimena said as they slogged through the suds. "What were you thinking?"

"I'm sorry," Serena repeated, but even as she spoke, a strange calm flowed over her and she no longer felt bad about what she had done. She watched Jimena from the corner of her eye. As soon as she was distracted, Serena escaped into the mountains of foam before Jimena could stop her.

When she came out of the bubbles on the other side, she saw Michael Saratoga, walking along the dry ledge, watching kids dance in the pit. She loved his dark angular features, his full sensual lips, captivating eyes, and spiked black hair. She had always had the feeling that if Vanessa weren't around, he would have called her. She smoothed her hands over her slick wet body and marched over to him.

"Hi, Michael," she said in an inviting voice. "Come join the party."

"I can't go in the foam," he said. "Band's playing. I have to stay dry."

She grabbed his hand anyway, enjoying the warm feel of his skin, and started to pull him forward.

"The band is performing in a few minutes," he said, eyes wary.

"I know you want to crawl into the bubbles with me," she coaxed.

He laughed, trying to pull his hand away, but she clutched his wrist. "What's got into you, Serena? You're acting so different."

"I've seen the way you look at me," she said, continuing to tug at him. "The way you're look-ing at me now."

Her body filled with fiery anticipation and she yanked hard. He lost his balance and tumbled into the suds. When he came up again, bubbles clung to his hair and shoulders, and he looked angry.

She pressed him back into a mound of foam, knowing she was too close, but his body felt too good to resist. "I can't let a gorgeous guy like you be wasted on Vanessa," she warned.

"Why'd you do that?" he asked, frowning.

"Because I need to kiss you," she answered, looking at him in a suggestive way, her hands smoothing up his chest.

"Vanessa's the only girl—" But before he could finish what he wanted to say, she plunged into his memories and hid all thoughts of Vanessa, along with his resistance.

With Vanessa erased from the front of his mind, he looked at Serena again as if seeing her for the first time. "You look hot tonight, Serena."

"Thanks." She loved her gift and wondered why she hadn't thought of doing this before. She was glad now for all the hours she had spent with Maggie, learning how to go inside people's minds and alter their thoughts.

Feeling Michael's desire, she smiled wickedly and pulled his face down to hers, a sweet yearning pulsing through her. "You've never been kissed by someone who kisses as good as I do," she whispered.

Soapsuds drizzled down her back as his hands slipped behind her, pressing her gently against him. She had closed her eyes and started to part her lips when someone grabbed her arm and yanked her away. She whipped around, then tripped and fell into the foam. She came up with a gasp and wiped the soap from her face.

"Are you *loca*, Serena?" Jimena demanded. "*¿Qué te pasa, chica?* What's got into you?"

Serena shuddered, and the world around her came back into sudden focus. She blinked and glanced at Michael standing in the foam, watching her with lovesick eyes.

"What were you doing?" Jimena asked.

Serena still felt confused. "I think I did something to mess with his mind."

Jimena stared at her in disbelief, then shook her head, spraying clumps of bubbles. "Fix it! He's got to go onstage and sing."

"Okay." Serena started to ease back inside his mind, but what she found made no sense to her. If she had curled his memories into this kind of tangle, she could no longer remember having done so. Worse, she wasn't sure how to unravel everything now. She left his thoughts as the DJ began announcing Michael's band. The drummer marked the beat, then the rhythm and lead guitars began to play.

Michael looked at them, his eyes suddenly alert. "I'm supposed to be onstage." He struggled through the foam.

"We better follow him." Serena started after him.

Serena and Jimena ran from the plastic tent, grabbing towels from the outstretched hands of the security guard.

"I hope he doesn't electrocute himself," Jimena said, wrapping the towel around her neck and watching the stage.

Vanessa held the microphone, waiting for Michael. He jumped on the stage, shook foam from his hair, picked up his guitar, pulled the strap over his head, and began to play.

Suddenly the band went full tilt into air-ripping music. Kids crowded the stage and Vanessa began to sing.

"Come on." Jimena nudged Serena. "Let's go, so we can talk."

When they were outside, walking toward the car, Serena shook her head. "What am I doing?" she asked, rubbing the towel through her hair.

"You're asking me?" Jimena demanded. "First you were kissing Derek, then you were all over Michael."

"I've never gone after another girl's guy, especially not the boyfriend of a friend." She started to shiver, and she didn't think it was from the cold alone.

"Foam parties make people do things they'd never do," Jimena said, but Serena knew she was only trying to cheer her up. "You just got more carried away than most."

Serena frowned. "No. It was something more than being in a party mood. It felt like someone else was making me use my power in ways I never would."

"Was it really that bad?" Jimena asked, snickering and putting her arm around Serena's shoulders. "Michael and Derek are two of the hottest guys at school."

"And Derek kisses fine." Serena glanced at Jimena, and they both broke out laughing.

People on the street turned to look at them.

"You should have seen the look on your face when you realized what you had done," Jimena said, gasping for air.

They fell against each other, uncontrollable laughter belting from them, and then as suddenly as it had started, the laughter was gone.

"I'm scared," Serena said in a low, trembling voice.

"Me too," Jimena whispered.

"What's happening to me?" Serena asked.

Jimena shook her head. "I'm not sure, but I don't think it's panic attacks or anything a medical doctor is going to be able to explain."

"I wish Maggie were here." Serena stared up at the sky, hidden now by the reflection of the glowing city lights. "When does she get home?"

"Not for another week at least," Jimena said, and then paused before pointing with her chin. "Look who Jerome found."

Serena turned. Jerome stood near the entrance, talking to Morgan. She wore a skimpy black top, slit in the front, baring a sliver of skin between the buttons, her micromini slung low on her hips, her shiny black boots accentuating her perfect legs.

"We need to talk to her." Jimena started walking back.

"Why?" Serena asked, following her.

"I don't know why yet," Jimena answered. "I just know that we do."

"It better be important." Serena wrapped the towel around her neck. "If I go up there, Jerome is going to think I'm jealous."

"Morgan!" Jimena called.

Morgan turned, her smile fading into fear.

Jerome looked up, an odd expression on his face, then he saw Serena and smiled.

"We need to talk to you," Jimena said to Morgan. "Alone."

"Look, I'm no longer part of it," Morgan said. Her smoky eye makeup made her eyes stand out.

"Part of what?" Jerome asked.

"It only concerns Morgan," Serena answered, taking Morgan's arm and pulling her away.

"Leave me alone, okay?" Morgan tried to shake free, but they didn't drop their hold. Reluctantly she went with them.

"You're hiding something," Jimena said, and stopped. "Something that you need to tell us."

"I don't know anything!" Morgan complained.

Serena narrowed her eyes and started to probe Morgan's mind, but then she felt Jimena's hand on her arm, cautioning her to stop.

"Tell us." Jimena's voice was soft and coaxing.

Morgan moved her lips as if she were trying to say what was on her mind. Then she stepped back into the hollow entrance of a brick building until she was hidden in shadow, her eyes studying the night behind them. Cars, trucks, and vans rumbled down the street, but most of the pedestrians were home now.

"All right," she warned. "I'll tell you, but it doesn't mean anything."

"I think it does," Jimena assured her.

"I'm trying to live like a regular kid again," Morgan insisted. "But I still sense things that are happening with the Followers. And lately I've been having dreams, and they're scaring me."

"Nightmares?" Jimena asked.

Morgan shook her head. "No. It's different. I go places, like to meetings. . . ." Her voice trailed off as if the memory of it were disturbing to her.

"What kind of meetings?" Serena asked, feeling a peculiar drop in her stomach as she sensed that what Morgan was having weren't dreams at all, but something hideously real.

Morgan's eyes brightened with tears.

"Tell us," Jimena urged again.

"I think somehow I've tapped into their world," Morgan said in a thin voice. "Some Followers are planning to overthrow the Atrox, and they're getting ready for the battle. There's going to be a war in the underworld." She looked from one to the other. "That's all I know."

Suddenly she darted between them and ran back to the foam party, leaving the sweet smell of her perfume in the air.

"Do you think she's telling the truth?" Serena asked, watching Morgan grab Jerome's arm and go inside with him.

"I don't know." Jimena shrugged. "She could be telling the truth, but even if she is, it doesn't mean she isn't being used by Followers to set a trap for us."

"I wish Maggie were here," Serena said for the second time that night.

"Me, too," Jimena agreed.

CHAPTER EIGHT

SATURDAY MORNING, Serena stood on the stage in the auditorium, kids in the school orchestra staring at her with wide-eyed disbelief. She had forgotten her cello.

"I don't understand why you bothered to come to practice if you didn't bring your instrument." Mr. Darby, the music director, stepped off the conductor's podium, the confusion on his pale face matching her own. His stringy brown hair fell across his glasses, hiding his eyes.

Serena pushed down a need to scream. Why hadn't she brought her cello with her? As hard as she tried, she couldn't remember why she had left it at home. "Can I stay and read the music while everyone plays?"

"Whoa!" Ollie, a senior, yelled from the back. "I've heard of someone playing the air guitar before, but never the air cello."

Laughter erupted around her, echoing from the stage out into the empty auditorium. Mr. Darby frowned and tapped his baton against the side of his leg. Silence followed, and kids began setting up silver music stands with loud clatters.

"I thought I left it at school," she lied defensively, pressing her hands against her face, wishing she could control the blush rising to her cheeks.

"Come with me, Serena." Mr. Darby walked with her to the wing of the stage, his footsteps thudding hollowly on the floor.

"I really am sorry," Serena tried again. "Couldn't I stay and help, Mr. Darby? There must be something I can do."

"You skipped a practice this week and now you've forgotten your cello," Mr. Darby said sternly, his pale blue eyes squinting. "Maybe you should reconsider performing with the orchestra. Lots of students lose interest once they discover how much they need to practice."

Her heart fell. "I love playing with the orchestra," she whispered, trying to sound contrite.

"I know you did at one time, but for right now it's better that you leave." He raised a thin eyebrow. "Your presence is distracting the others."

She glanced back. Ollie sat in a folding chair, knees spread around an imaginary cello, his head bent, hands mimicking Serena running a bow over the strings.

"My solo?" she asked, her lower lip trembling.

Mr. Darby took a deep breath and she knew a lecture was building.

She cut in before he could start. "I'll practice twice as much next week."

Mr. Darby ran the end of the baton into his hair, scratching his scalp with the tip. Finally he smiled, showing an even row of teeth. "We'll start with a clean slate next week. Fair enough?"

Serena nodded and walked to the exit,

rubbing the back of her neck against the headache building there. She drew a long, shaky breath and pushed outside, then turned, watching the gray metal door slam shut. She waited, hoping Mr. Darby would change his mind at the last moment and let her stay.

When the sounds of the orchestra grew louder, she walked away, feeling disheartened and a little frightened. Her life was beginning to feel like a nightmare. She hadn't turned in any home-work this past week, and now her solo was up in the air. She was going to go home and start in on her history assignment, then practice her cello twice as hard and prove to Mr. Darby that she was dedicated.

But at the front gate entrance she paused, her fingers clutching the wire mesh fence as a sudden calm came over her.

The water polo team practiced on Saturday morning. How could she forget something as important as that? She smiled, thinking of Michael. He was on the team. Suddenly she felt better and wondered why she had been so worried about homework and missing another practice. She could make up everything next week. Right now she had something more important she needed to do.

She turned and ran back across the tarmac, the intense need to see Michael building inside her. When she reached the boys' locker room, she peered into the dark entrance, the odors of mildew and sweat floating around her. She hoped she wasn't too late.

Running footsteps filled the silence, and Michael darted out, almost colliding with her, his chest bare, hair still wet and dripping on his shoulders. His perfect dark eyes looked at her curiously, as if memories of last night were too clear in his mind.

"Hi, Michael," she said, breathing in the chlorine and soap smells clinging to him. She caught a drop of water running down his chest with the tip of her finger and held it up, tilting her head. "You forgot to dry off."

"Do you need to see me about something?" he asked bluntly.

"Just wanted to say hi," she answered in a sultry voice that didn't sound like her own.

"Hey." He nodded and kept walking, but he didn't seem too upset or angry with her over last night.

She took that as a good sign. Good sign! What was she thinking? He was Vanessa's boyfriend. She tried to stop herself from following him, but her feet became suddenly unmanageable dead iron weights no longer under her control. She staggered, unsure, her breath catching, and grabbed the edge of a bicycle rack to keep from falling. The beige stucco wall behind her seemed to tilt and sway. Her vision narrowed, then an odd sensation swept over her, as if she were detaching from her body and being pushed to the back of her head, an outsider observing.

"Michael," she called, reaching for him, her voice trembling. "I think I'm going to faint."

He turned sharply, alarm in his eyes, and ran back to her, catching her as she crumpled to the ground. He propped her against him, his eyes moving from side to side, looking for someone to help.

Her cheek rested against his broad chest, listening to the steady thump of his heart, then she watched with a mixture of shock and fascination as her hands smoothed over his bare skin. She must be in a trance or dreaming, maybe even under the influence of some strange disease or drug, because it felt as if another personality were replacing her own.

"I think I'm okay now," she whispered.

Serena couldn't believe the girlie-girl way she was holding her head and looking up at Michael. She might as well be batting her eyelashes. Her hands brushed up his arms, her fingers enjoying the feel of his rock-hard muscles.

"You sure?" he asked.

"Yes. I'm glad you were here." Her words echoed inside her as if someone else were speaking through her lips.

"I'll give you a ride home." His frown told her he was worried.

That was all the encouragement she needed. With rising horror, she sensed the next words forming in her mouth. "I never got my—" She bit her tongue to keep herself from asking Michael for the kiss she didn't get the night before.

"Never got what?" Michael asked, staring at her with his gorgeous distressed eyes. "Did you forget to take some medicine?"

"That's not what I need," she said.

Serena tried to plunge into his mind and tell him what was happening to her, but with a jolt she realized she no longer had control over her power, either. Her heart raced. She watched helplessly as her hands inched up Michael's chest and encircled his neck, her lips parting for the kiss.

"What do you need?" Michael looked at her with real concern.

Frantic, she tried to scream to warn him away, but no sound came from her throat. Was she going to spend the rest of her life locked in her own body, unable to communicate or control her actions?

CHAPTER NINE

A

S SUDDENLY AS it had come, the odd hypnotic state was gone. Serena slammed back into her body with a jolt, an ear-piercing scream ripping from her throat.

Michael flinched, a startled expression on his face. He dropped his hold and jerked back. When he let go, she stumbled, hitting her head on the wall. What had just happened to her? She felt as if she had been someone else for a moment.

"Serena, do you need to go to the hospital?" Michael grabbed her arm again to steady her.

She pulled away, frantically searching for an

excuse. "Well, I hope you came up with an idea."

"Idea?" He looked at her oddly.

"Yeah, I was trying to give you inspiration for a new song, like *Go away, girl, I belong to someone else!*" She tried to laugh, but tears brimmed and she stopped, fearful one giggle would release a ceaseless stream of tears. What was she going to do? Vanessa would freak when Michael told her that Serena had been trying to kiss him again.

She sighed. "Sorry, Michael. I didn't mean—"

"It's all right," he whispered.

"All right?" she asked in disbelief.

"You don't need to be embarrassed about it," he said.

"I don't?" she asked, feeling confused. "Why not?"

"Vanessa told me you were having panic attacks." He brushed her hair from her eyes in a brotherly way.

"Is that what you think happened?" she asked.

He nodded.

She wrinkled her nose and sniffed, holding

back the tears. Maybe it was better to leave things alone and let him believe that.

"I better go," she said quietly.

"Are you all right now?"

She nodded as Jerome came from the locker room. He saw her and waved. "Hey, Serena, wait up."

"Gotta go, Jerome," she yelled, glancing down at her watch. "I told Collin I'd meet him at the beach."

Today had been a total bust, and there was no way she was going to add Jerome to the mix. She turned to leave, her legs still tingling from the dead heaviness she had felt earlier. Now she was going to go home and crawl into bed. Her head was killing her.

She glanced back. Michael and Jerome were talking, their arms moving as if they were reliving moments from their water polo practice. She had never believed a guy was the answer, but now she was beginning to wonder. Perhaps she did need a boyfriend. She couldn't continue attacking her friends' boyfriends. Maybe her hormones were out of whack. Did such things even happen? Yet with every embarrassing thing that had taken place, she still wondered what Michael would have done if she had kissed him.

She made her way across the tarmac, falling deeper and deeper into her thoughts.

The sudden flapping of pigeons startled into flight brought her back. She flinched as the birds took off, downy feathers falling around her. She turned slowly, wondering how she could have walked into a flock of pigeons without being aware of it, and then with a start she realized she was at the bus stop already.

She looked back over her shoulder. She couldn't remember walking here. Then an odd feeling came over her. The morning light seemed somehow different, the sun high in the sky now. She glanced at her watch.

"Twelve noon," she whispered in disbelief, and sat on the bench.

With a shock, she realized two hours had passed. How could she lose track of time like that? She closed her eyes, trying to gather her thoughts, but the last two hours remained a blank to her.

When she opened her eyes again, she saw a Lexus parked down the other side of the street. She stood and squinted, bringing her vision into better focus. The designer plates read STAR. The driver's side window was down, and an old woman wearing jet-black sunglasses was looking back as if she were watching Serena. She had to be the same woman Serena had collided with in the alley.

Serena didn't know why the woman had been following her, but she was determined to find out. She dodged into the bumper-to-bumper traffic that always cruised Melrose on Saturday and darted behind a FedEx delivery truck waiting for the streetlight to turn green. She used it for cover, then ducked behind a Chevy loaded with kids her own age.

She crouched low, her hand resting on the shimmying back bumper. Exhaust fumes curled into her nose, gagging her.

She continued down the street, hiding

behind the cars stopped for the red light, until she was even with the Lexus. She peered over the trunk of a yellow Buick.

The woman in the Lexus was straining her neck, looking back as if searching for Serena.

When the light changed to green, the cars started to roll. Serena dashed in front of a utility van and sprinted across the street to the Lexus. She slapped her hands on the roof.

The woman recoiled, then slowly lifted her shades and stared at Serena with a contemptuous grin, her large gold earrings dangling to her shoulders. Blue veins were visible through the skin on her chest.

"Why are you following me?" Serena asked.

Traffic buzzed behind her, creating a breeze that ruffled her hair.

"I wanted to give you something." The woman reached across the car seat and handed Serena a brown Macy's bag. "I have a present for you."

Serena kept her hands on the rooftop. "Why would you give me anything? I don't even know you."

"Take it." She shoved the bag at Serena.

Cautiously she did.

"Open it." The woman stretched her hand out the window and impatiently ripped at the white tissue wrapping with her red-dagger nails, pulling it free. It blew away, flying down the street.

A bottle of Joy perfume and two jars of Estée Lauder face cream sat in the bottom of the brown bag.

"Why are you giving me these?" Serena asked.

"Your skin has been looking a little blotchy lately and you'll love the perfume," the woman said, her fingers working around her car keys.

"What makes you think I'll like the perfume?" Serena asked.

"Because I love it!" she said with a loud laugh, then, stabbing the key into the ignition, she turned the starter. The motor purred to life.

Serena tried to penetrate the woman's thoughts before she drove off, but all she picked up were her own memories and dreams. How was that possible? Did the woman have some kind of mind control of her own? Maybe she knew how to deflect Serena's power. She didn't look like a Follower, but that didn't mean she wasn't one.

"Buh-bye!" The woman waved her hand out the window, the sun catching the heavy jewels on her fingers. Then she stomped the accelerator.

Serena jumped back as the car shot away from the curb with a squeal of tires. Dust blew around her, and the smell of burning rubber filled the air.

As Serena watched the Lexus zip into traffic and run a red light, her chest filled with a helpless rage. She was certain now that whatever was happening to her was somehow connected to the woman.

CHAPTER TEN

CATTY SAT IN THE chair next to Serena's bed, reading the label on the jar of face cream. The pink rhinestones embellishing her low-rise pants shimmered in the late afternoon sunlight coming through the windows.

"It's the same stuff my mom uses." Vanessa took the jar from Catty, unscrewed the lid, lifted a plastic shield, and smelled the contents before touching the cream with the tip of her finger. "It seems okay to me."

Tianna sprayed the perfume, sniffing the

rose-and-jasmine fragrance. "The perfume smells good."

"I don't think we should breathe that stuff." Jimena opened the balcony doors, letting in a cool breeze. The drapes swirled, undulating in the puffing air.

"Why not?" Catty asked, adjusting the shoulder strap on her halter.

"Serena's been having panic attacks and blackouts since that woman made her drink the water," Jimena explained. "Maybe she added something dangerous to the creams and perfume."

"Like some kind of designer drug?" Tianna set the bottle of perfume on the desk with a faint clank, her eyes wide with sudden alarm.

"The packages were sealed," Serena said, snuggling deeper under her covers. She had spent most of the day in bed, doing the homework she should have completed the week before.

"Like they can't be opened and resealed?" Jimena rolled her eyes.

"Maybe we should stay with Serena and not go

out." Vanessa sprawled on the bottom of the bed.

"I don't want to stop you guys from going." Serena sat up suddenly. She didn't like the apprehension she saw on her friends' faces. "Whatever's going on, I can handle it."

"Then forget about the old woman and come with us," Tianna said.

"Come clubbing," Catty pleaded. "Everyone's talking about the new place in the Valley. Besides, you know you'd be safer with us."

Serena shook her head. "Until I figure out what's wrong with me, I know I'll feel safer at home."

"You mean the guys are safer with you at home," Jimena teased, trying to lighten Serena's mood.

"I think one of us should stay with Serena," Vanessa said.

"I don't need a baby-sitter," Serena insisted.

When they didn't move, she threw back her covers, swung her legs over the edge of the bed, and stood. She walked to her bedroom door with determined steps and opened it. "If you don't go, you'll make me feel like something is seriously wrong with me."

Vanessa bit the side of her cheek as if deciding.

Finally Catty got up, shrugged, and walked to the hallway. "But you call us on my cell phone if anything happens."

"I won't need to," Serena reassured her.

Reluctantly they left.

A few minutes later Serena was back in bed, history book propped against her knees. She had been studying for an hour or more when a strange dizziness came over her. She tried to get out of bed, but her legs buckled, and she plopped back on the edge of her mattress, feeling inexplicably tired. She dropped onto her pillow and closed her eyes.

Hours later a police siren startled Serena awake. Fast-moving white lights buzzed at her, making her blink. In a flash she realized she wasn't in her bed anymore but walking down a street, a chilly breeze snapping around her, the glare of headlights from the speeding squad car shining in her eyes. The police car blasted past her and disappeared, leaving her in silence.

She clasped her throat with icy fingers and looked down the empty, trash-strewn sidewalk in stunned disbelief. She didn't know where she was or how she had gotten here.

It had to be a dream, but she knew it wasn't. Her body shivered violently, teeth chattering, as if she had been outside in the cold for a long time. She became aware of a foul taste in her mouth and shuddered, wondering what she had eaten. She had no recollection of where she had been or what she had been doing.

She needed to catch a bus home or find a pay phone and call Collin. She pressed her hands against her hips, searching for pockets with money, and suddenly felt naked. She glanced down at her clothing. She was wearing an unfamiliar, clingy see-through shell and a low-slung miniskirt. She took an uneasy step back, turning as she did, her spiked heels scraping against the concrete walk, and eased into the shadows of a weather shelter hanging over a bus bench. She started to sit, but a homeless man lay on the long seat, swaddled in newspapers. She leaned against the back wall, staring out at the night.

The street sign read ALVARADO. She glanced at the storefront buildings. RITMO LATINO. PULGARITA. All the advertisements were in Spanish. She must be somewhere in the Pico-Union District of Los Angeles. That gave her a feeling of hope. If she could find Wilshire Boulevard, she could find Jimena's apartment.

She was about to start walking when pounding music shattered the night. A Ford Torino turned the corner and wheeled down the street, its music booming through her. She ducked behind the snoring homeless man and watched the carload of bangers, scoping out their neighborhood.

When the car screeched away, she stood, knowing she needed to find safety quickly. She glanced both ways, then kicked off her spiked sandals and ran barefoot down the sidewalk toward MacArthur Park.

She hurried past Langer's Deli, then made a

diagonal sprint through the intersection. She entered the park, leaping over the makeshift shelters of the homeless before her feet found the path circling the lake. Tiny pebbles cut into her soles, but she didn't alter her pace. Her arms continued pumping at her sides.

Normally a fountain sprayed a column of water into the air, but it was off now. That meant the hour was even later than she had first assumed. She glanced at the eastern sky. Already the edge of night was turning gray with the approach of dawn.

At Wilshire Boulevard she bolted through the intersection, each breath now a painful draw, her muscles burning with the need for oxygen, but instead of slowing she raced to the brick apartment building where Jimena lived with her grandmother.

She hurried past the cement lions sitting on either side of the porch steps and pressed her finger on the call button, then rested her head against the metal panel and didn't release her hold until Jimena's angry voice answered.

"*¡Déjate tocando! ¡Basta ya!*"

"It's me, Jimena," Serena said into the inter-com, through gasps for air.

"Serena?" Jimena's baffled voice whispered as the buzzer sounded, releasing the magnetic lock.

Serena slipped inside. A dusty light illumi-nated the long spiraling stairs leading up from the old hotel lobby. She limped carefully down the hall to a small elevator, the soles of her feet sting-ing, a cut on her big toe bleeding, and rode up to Jimena's floor.

When the metal door opened, Jimena was waiting for her. The somber expression on her face was quickly replaced by one of surprise. "I thought you didn't want to go clubbing," Jimena said.

Serena shook her head, tears suddenly becoming stronger than her ability to hold them back.

"*¿Estás llorando?*" Jimena wrapped a comfort-ing arm around her, her warmth seeping into Serena's cold skin as they walked down the gloomy hallway. "Why are you crying?"

Jimena's grandmother stood in the open

doorway, a small silhouette against the light inside. She moved aside, letting them enter, her black eyes anxious, then closed the door behind them and disappeared into the kitchen.

Serena sat on the couch, rubbing her arms. The air was warm inside and smelled of onions, chili peppers, and spice.

"What happened to you, *chica*?" Jimena pulled a yellow-and-red hand-knitted comforter from the arm of a chair and wrapped it around Serena.

"I don't know," Serena answered, unable to stop the shivering.

"Just tell me what you do know," Jimena said, sitting beside her.

Jimena's grandmother reappeared, carrying a cup of warm tea. *"Es sonámbula,"* she said, and sat across from them, the beads of her rosary carefully moving between her fingers.

"What did she say?" Serena asked, wiping at her eyes before sipping the sweet tea.

"She says you're a sleepwalker," Jimena explained.

"I had to have been sleepwalking," Serena

agreed. "It's the only explanation."

"All the way over here?" Jimena asked, pinching the edge of Serena's flimsy miniskirt. "Usually you don't get all made up like a hoochie mama to go sleepwalking."

"I know," Serena answered softly, feeling something inside her give in. "I'm wearing *her* perfume." She lifted her wrist for Jimena to smell.

Jimena breathed the fragrance, her eyes becoming more worried.

They stared at each other in stunned silence.

"*La llorona*," Jimena's grandmother whispered.

"What?" Serena asked.

"It's one of my grandmother's shiver stories," Jimena said

"Tell me."

"The crying lady lures people to their death because St. Peter won't let her into heaven until she finds the souls of her sons," Jimena explained. "So she steals the souls from other people, like someone out walking alone late at night, and takes their soul up to heaven to show St. Peter, hoping he'll let her in."

"You think someone's trying to steal my soul?" Serena looked in Jimena's eyes, expecting to find comfort there, but instead she saw fear.

"Of course not," Jimena answered. "We just don't have the answer yet."

"Stay with me until we do," Serena whispered. "I'm scared."

CHAPTER ELEVEN

Later that morning, Serena and Jimena went over to Borders on La Cienega. They sat next to the upstairs window, the Sunday *LA Times* spread on the table in front of them. The steam rising from their chai teas scented the air with the soothing aromas of ginger, cloves, and cinnamon. They spent hours going over the night before, struggling to find some trace of memory that might unlock what had happened to Serena.

Even though they had found no clue, by the end of the afternoon Serena felt better. They ate Reese's peanut-butter cups with chocolate ice cream for dinner, then, after watching the ten o'clock news, they went upstairs to Serena's bedroom.

Serena sat on her bed, wrapping a fresh Band-Aid around the cut on her toe.

"If you start sleepwalking, you'll step on me first," Jimena said, joking, and spread a red sleeping bag beside Serena's bed.

Serena pulled on a green nightshirt and snuggled under her covers, feeling drowsy. "I really appreciate your staying with me all day."

"Don't get mushy on me," Jimena warned, slipping into a Lakers T-shirt. She had planned to go to the game that night at the Staples Center with Collin.

"But I ruined your plans," Serena said guiltily.

"We'll go to the next game." Jimena switched off the overhead light.

Shadows crowded into the room. Serena leaned on her elbow, studying the dark.

Jimena glanced down at her moon amulet. "Nothing is there," she said, crawling into her sleeping bag. "Besides, I got your back."

"Thanks," Serena said, but before she could finish telling Jimena how grateful she felt, sleep took her.

In the blurred images of a dream Serena found herself walking down Sunset Boulevard toward the Dungeon, a club where Followers hung out. She crossed the parking lot to the two-story beige building, the tap of her stiletto heels echoing behind her. Her moon amulet throbbed against her chest, warning her of danger, but she continued anyway. Her hands grabbed the smooth brass door handle, and she slipped inside.

Her vision took a long time to adjust to the dark, and when she could finally see again, she realized she was staring into the mirrored panels near the door, dusting a frosty gray shadow over her lids. Her eyes looked provocative and catlike, glinting with amber lights. She felt mesmerized by her own reflection, her beauty looking flawless and pure evil now.

The music changed and she turned, scanning the bar and the low couches against the wall. With a shock she realized that in this upside-down fantasyland she had come to the Dungeon to party. She pushed into the crowded dance floor until she was sandwiched between two Followers who had once been her enemies. Her hips swayed, dancing against them. It felt so real, and the smells of cigarette smoke, sweat and perfume seemed too vivid.

Tymmie shoved through the throng of moving arms and legs. He had once been apprenticed to Stanton, but since Stanton had become Prince of Night, Tymmie had started using guns and fists as well as his new power as a shape-changer to spread evil. He flaunted what he was now, and in this world of dreams she admired his boldness.

"I thought you'd never get here," he said, as if he had been waiting for her.

Her amulet shot menacing white light into his eyes. Tymmie grinned and lifted her charm, then pinched the top of her halter, pulling it out. He dropped the talisman inside. A faint glow still shone through the see-through material, but it didn't seem to bother him as much now. He held up his thumb, showing off the moon image her amulet had burned into his skin.

"So, what took you so long?" he asked, pulling her against him and starting to dance.

In spite of herself she pressed next to him, her hands rubbing over his shaved head. He had tattooed ATROX on his scalp.

"You'll have to get rid of that," she teased.

He tore away from her, turning, and lifted his shirt. INFIDUS was tattooed in bright red, green, and blue inks across the small of his back. Fear rose in her throat. *Infidi* in Latin meant "the treacherous ones," but she was certain the word stood for something more in the hierarchy of the Atrox. She tried to shoot inside his mind to see, but in this dream world her psychic ability didn't work.

"Here comes your boyfriend," Tymmie teased.

She followed his look. Jerome joined the fantasy now, elbowing his way through the swinging arms and heads.

"Let's dance." Jerome forced her close to him, his desire unmasked.

She didn't want to dance with him, but in the churning nighttime vision she lifted her hands over her head, her body moving sinuous and slow against him. She dropped her hands around his neck and stared into his eyes, but it felt as if she were looking at him through a veil.

"I knew I'd have you one day." Jerome gazed back at her with frank sexual suggestion, his hands dangerously bold. "I just didn't realize what I'd have to do to get you."

What did you have to do? she tried to ask, but instead of words, a laugh trickled from her throat, high and shrill, not like her own.

The music stopped and she pulled him back to the chairs along the wall. They sat down and she flung up her legs, resting her feet on his lap. He took off her shoes as if he did it all the time, and began rubbing her bare ankles, his fingers continuing up to her calves, caressing and slow.

"I don't want anyone else to dance with you," he said.

"Then how are you going to mark me so everyone will know I belong to you?" Serena asked coyly.

He grabbed a felt marker someone had left on a nearby stool. "I'll write my name on you."

She felt deliciously wicked as he lifted her skirt and the tip of the marker tickled her thigh. He wrote JEROME over her skin in cold black ink, then smiled when he was done.

"Come on," he said quietly, slipping her shoes back onto her feet.

"Where are we going?" she asked as he pulled her up.

"I'm going to take you to another party," he announced. "The one you've been wanting to go to."

She nodded, knowing in a strange way the other party was where she was supposed to be.

The dream seemed to fade then, and when she opened her eyes again, the night was spinning around her in a kaleidoscope of flashing lights. They were speeding recklessly down the Hollywood Freeway in Jerome's Camaro. Cold air rumbled through the open windows, slapping her hair into her face. Her heart raced with sudden fear as he looped onto the Long Beach Freeway, squeezing between two fast-moving trucks. She was a goddess, but not immortal.

With a sudden swerve he took an off-ramp into the City of Commerce and jammed on the brakes. The car fishtailed wildly, and for a moment she thought he was going to lose control, but then the car slowed and they drove past rows of warehouses and factories, the smells of oil, smoke, and petroleum distillate filling the air.

Finally Jerome parked and took her hand.

"You'll like this party, Serena," he said. "It's for you." He cupped a hand around her neck.

She slid closer to him, and in the dream she felt her hands touch him as if she had been waiting to kiss him for a long time. He smiled at her in a crooked sort of way, sensing her desire, but he didn't move to kiss her. Instead he opened his car door and climbed out, pulling her after him.

"Let me show you first," he whispered against her cheek, then, taking her hand, he led her toward an abandoned factory.

As they got closer, the repetitive hypnotic beat of the electronic dance music grew louder. When they slipped inside, Followers ran to her, calling her by a name she had never heard before. Some even hugged her, their faces haunted in the flashing strobe light.

Jerome put his arm around her waist and pulled her away from the crowd. Over his shoulder she studied the faces of the dancers, knowing something was different about these Followers. The girls wore low-slung slacks, lashes with glitter, and rhinestone eyelid jewels. Crystal tattoos circled their navels in iridescent reds and blues, the word *infidus* tattooed over their hipbones.

"They wear the mark of the traitor," Jerome whispered against her ear, as if he had sensed her question. "All of them. The Followers here all want to overthrow the Atrox. We're loyal to Lambert."

"Lambert?" she asked, finally finding her

voice. "Lambert is imprisoned in Stanton's memories."

"I know, but you'll free him for us, won't you, Serena?" Jerome looked at her as if he knew she would.

She struggled desperately to wake up. She needed to warn Stanton, but the nightmare held her, becoming more gray and distant. She tumbled deeper and deeper into this phantom nocturnal world until it swallowed her.

Milky light from an overcast morning woke Serena. Outside, sparrows perched on the balcony railing, chirping wildly. She opened her eyes, thankful to find herself still in bed, nestled under warm covers. She stretched, breathing the aroma of coffee and bacon, her chest filling with a warm sense of gratitude that last night had only been a bad dream.

She leaned on her elbow and glanced over the side of the bed. Jimena was deep in slumber, her arms twisted around her pillow.

"Jimena?" Serena nudged her.

She sat up with a start, alert and ready. Her head jerked around, and when she saw Serena looking at her, she relaxed.

"You didn't go anywhere last night," Jimena said in triumph.

"Sleepwalking might have been better than the nightmare I had." Serena rested her head in her hands.

Jimena leaned back on the pillow. "Tell me."

"I was at the Dungeon, dancing with Tymmie and Jerome," Serena said, but the dream was fading rapidly.

"So what's so bad about that?" Jimena teased. "You love to dance."

Serena shuddered. "It was one of those nightmares where you know it's a dream, but you still can't wake up."

Jimena laughed.

"What?" Serena asked.

"Before I met you," Jimena said, "I knew I was wide awake, but I kept praying for my life to be only a nightmare, *una pesadilla*, so I could wake up and live like everyone else without worrying every day if I was going to get blasted."

Serena stared at her friend. Jimena had been one badass homegirl before Maggie had introduced them. She had even been sentenced twice to Youth Authority Camp for jacking cars.

Jimena stood suddenly and pulled on a fluffy pink robe with giant yellow flowers. It had been a gift from Collin. "You wait here. I'll go get us some coffee."

"Say good morning to Collin for me." Serena smiled slyly as Jimena ducked into the hallway.

Serena lingered in bed a few minutes, deciding what she would wear to school, then threw back her covers, swung her feet over the side, and glanced down. New blisters covered her toes, and the Band-Aid she had wrapped around her big toe the night before was missing.

Her heart raced. She pinched the hem of her green nightshirt, slowly lifting it above her knees. In disbelief, she stared down at JEROME written in black marker across her thigh.

CHAPTER TWELVE

A FEW MOMENTS LATER Jimena walked into the bedroom, humming happily, two steaming yellow mugs of coffee balanced in her hands, a piece of toast stuck between her teeth. She glanced at Serena, and in one smooth movement she set the coffees on the desk, took the toast from her mouth, tossed it in the trash, and walked over to the bed, her eyes never leaving the letters scrawled over Serena's leg.

"No es posible," she said to herself. Finally she looked at Serena. "You couldn't have gotten out of bed without waking me."

"Unless I was awake," Serena said, "and

knew what I was doing. Remember what Zahi could do to me?"

Jimena nodded.

Zahi was a powerful Follower who had been able to put Serena in a trance, controlling her thoughts without her having any memory of it.

"Maggie will be back in less than a week." Jimena sat on the bed next to her. "We'll get some answers then."

"It will be too late by then," Serena answered.

"How do you know?" Jimena asked, her dark eyes filled with worry.

"I just do," Serena whispered. "I can feel a pressure building inside my head. Something's there, and it's growing stronger."

Jimena stood abruptly, walked over to the closet, tore a pair of jeans from a hanger, and threw them at Serena. "Get dressed," she ordered, stripping off her robe. "We're going to go see Jerome before he has a chance to run off to school."

"He's the last person I want to see," Serena said, slumping back on her pillow.

Jimena gazed at her with fierce determination. "We're going to ask him what he knows."

Serena sat up, grabbed the waistband of her jeans, and slid a leg inside. A smile crossed her lips. "And if he won't tell us, I'll read his mind, no matter how disgusting his thoughts are."

When they were dressed, Jimena tore a page from the telephone book and they ran outside, then headed toward Jerome's house at a fast, even clip. Soon they were walking down his street.

"Ready?" Jimena opened a blue gate set between two hedges of Arizona cypress.

Serena nodded and followed Jimena into the yard, her tension rising as they stepped down a narrow stone walk to Jerome's front porch. Geraniums sat in terra-cotta pots near the door.

Jimena rang the doorbell. It chimed inside.

The door opened immediately, and a short woman in a blue robe with uncombed blond hair stood in front of them, her eyes puffy, as if she had been crying. "Yes?"

"Could we speak to Jerome?"

The woman collapsed against the doorjamb, her expression desperate. "He didn't come home last night," she whispered, her chin quivering. "That isn't like him. He always helps me set up at the restaurant before he goes to school. I know something has happened to him."

"Maybe you should call the police and let them know he's missing," Serena said softly, sure now that Tymmie had turned Jerome to the Atrox.

The woman nodded, her lower lip pulling into a tight, thin smile. "I'm sure he'll be home soon," she said, more to herself than Serena. "He probably just had car trouble."

"Do you want us to stay with you?" Jimena offered.

She shook her head and closed the door. They could hear her sobbing as they walked away.

"Assuming my dream was real," Serena began.

"Do you have any doubt?" Jimena asked.

"None," Serena answered with certainty. "Then that means that both Jerome and Tymmie are hooked up with a new group of Followers. They call themselves *infidi*."

"*Infidi*," Jimena repeated. "The treacherous ones."

Serena nodded slowly, considering, as they walked through the spray from someone's automatic sprinklers. "Whatever is happening has to be connected to that old woman in the Lexus."

"We'll find her, then," Jimena said with confidence.

"How?" Serena asked. "The last time I tried to get some answers from her, she drove off."

"I haven't jacked a car for a long time." Jimena stretched her fingers as if she were anxious to try again.

"What does that have to do with it?"

"Next time she comes around, we'll jack her car and make her tell us what she knows."

Serena stared at Jimena. She was serious.

"No guns," Serena whispered, suddenly uneasy but for a new reason. She was about to break the law.

"Of course, no guns." Jimena smirked. "That would violate my probation."

"All right," Serena agreed finally. "But if I'm wrong, we could both end up in jail."

CHAPTER THiRTEEN

By the time Serena and Jimena arrived at Planet Bang, the club was already crowded with kids waiting to hear Michael's band. Smoky mist shot into the air, and lights blazed in a show as the DJ finished and his tech crew started packing. Michael's band had already set up and they were on the stage now, tuning and testing the microphones.

Serena scanned the room, looking for Jerome. Jimena stood beside her in khakis and

Doc Martens, the pockets of her navy-blue parka bulging with tools. When security had tried to confiscate her hammer and screwdriver, she had darted away before they could and sneaked in through the stage entrance.

Catty joined them, an orange fur-trimmed sweater coat wrapped around her silky skirt and top. "Have you seen Jerome?"

Both Jimena and Serena shook their heads.

"No one has seen him for two days now," Serena said. "I called his mother this afternoon and she still hasn't heard anything from him."

"I wish the old woman in the Lexus would show up so we could find out what's going on." Catty glanced at the stage.

"Me, too," Serena agreed. She was impatient to get it over. She had worn a long-sleeved purple tee, loose-fitting jeans, and combat boots. She didn't know what to expect from tonight.

Suddenly kids pressed forward, whooping and applauding wildly.

Vanessa walked across the stage and took the microphone, looking tall and slinky in a long olive cotton camouflage skirt, her tan legs peeking from the slits up the side.

Derek and Tianna pushed through the crowd to join them. Tianna wore a zip-front tank top, her hair straight and falling on her bare shoulders. Derek whispered something to her, and then they both looked up at Serena as if they were waiting to see what she would do.

Serena breathed a sigh of relief when she didn't feel that strange compulsion to touch Derek or flirt with him.

Vanessa began to sing and Serena froze. She had forgotten that Vanessa had asked if she could use her poem "Demon Lover" for the lyrics to her new song. Now hearing the words come from Vanessa's throaty voice made old emotions stir inside her. She glanced at the shadows in the back, looking for a sliver of night, wondering if Stanton was there. If he heard the song, he would know she had written the words.

"Let's go." Jimena nudged her.

"In the middle of Vanessa's song?" Serena asked, surprised.

Jimena lifted her chin, motioning toward the exit. "I don't know why yet, but we need to be on the street."

Serena shoved through the crowd after Jimena, hurrying toward the exit.

A few kids stood in the cool air outside, some dancing to the music flowing from inside, others laughing in groups. The huge neon Planet Bang sign pulsed, flashing pink, blue, green, and orange lights.

Serena joined Jimena on the curb. Above them banners hanging from the streetlights flapped lazily, advertising the LA Opera. The smoky smell of frying hamburgers came from a distant restaurant, but Serena didn't sense anything wrong. She followed Jimena's gaze, surveying a two-story stucco hotel and the cars parked in front.

"What are you looking for?" Serena asked, but before she had finished the question, she knew. She could feel the woman nearby.

Jimena touched her lightly, drawing her back behind two girls who were flirting with one of the security guards.

"Check it out," Jimena whispered, crouching.

The Lexus was parked at the corner on the far side of the street.

"I can't see through the windows," Serena complained. "Do you think she's inside?"

"Don't use your power," Jimena warned. "She might be able to sense you pushing into her mind."

Jimena stepped back, pulling Serena with her toward the entrance. When they were hidden in shadows, she stopped. "Do you remember everything I told you?"

"It could be dangerous," Serena answered, looking at the impossible distance they had to run to the car before the woman drove away.

"Yeah," Jimena said, a smile breaking across her face. "It could be." Her hands breezed over the pockets of her parka as if taking inventory.

Serena nodded, her heart already starting to pound. "Then let's hit it."

They bolted across the sidewalk, their feet thundering across the concrete. Kids turned and stared at them as they shot between the parked cars, leaping recklessly into the street without checking the oncoming traffic. A car honked, barely missing Jimena. Her palm went down flat on the hood and she used it to spring over the bumper as if she had done it a hundred times before.

Serena didn't let the near collision stop her. She streaked down the street, dodging approaching cars, eyes steady on her target, arms pumping at her sides.

Inside Planet Bang, Michael's band started a new song with a quick and loud beat. The music spilled into the night, and the frantic rhythm seemed to match the speed of Serena's heart.

The engine of the Lexus roared to life, exhaust spitting from the tailpipe.

"She's seen us!" Serena shouted, but didn't stop running. Jimena had warned her that this would happen, but Serena hadn't anticipated it taking place so quickly. With a burst of energy she tore at an angle toward the right side of the car, adrenaline raging through her body.

The car lurched forward, but before it pulled

away from the curb, Jimena swung her hammer and cracked the glass. She swung again. This time gummy pebbles of black glass flew, showering the street and the inside of the car. Jimena dropped the hammer. It hit the pavement with a solid clank, and she shot her hand inside, her fingers grabbing the steering wheel, guiding the car toward the curb.

Serena rushed through the cloud of exhaust, circling to the passenger side and gripped the door handle. It tugged away from her as the front wheels bumped over the curb, then down again with a bounce.

"It's locked," Serena shouted. Her hands were sweating so badly, she wasn't sure she'd be able to open the door even if it were unlocked.

Jimena flipped the master lock.

When the lock popped up, Serena yanked open the door, slid inside, and slammed her foot on the brake. The car jolted to a stop. She grabbed the gearshift and forced it into park. The noise of grinding metals followed, and then the car shuddered and stalled. Serena yanked the keys from the ignition, clutching them tightly in her shaking fingers.

"Serena!" Jimena shouted in warning.

She looked up. The woman pointed a gun at her. Her heart felt as if it were going to explode.

With one smooth movement Jimena opened the car door, shoved in next to the woman, and tore the gun from her hand.

"Don't!" Terror ripped through Serena as she wondered what Jimena planned to do next.

Jimena smiled fiercely, then pulled the clip from the gun and slipped both under the seat.

Serena rubbed at her chest, willing her heart to slow, and watched the woman, wondering why she wasn't afraid of them. Instead she patted her dry, coarse tar-black hair and glanced in the rearview mirror, rubbing her small finger around the lipstick smeared over her thin, pale lips.

"My friend's got something she wants to ask you," Jimena said, her eyes flashing menacingly.

The woman turned with an amused grin and looked at Serena.

"Why have you been following me?" Serena asked, hating the unsure sound in her voice.

"Because we're trading bodies," the woman stated simply.

"Right," Jimena said bluntly. "Answer her question."

"Serena knows it's true," the woman went on. "Don't you, Serena?"

Serena grabbed the dashboard, blood rushing and pulsing through her head as sudden vertigo made the world slant.

"It's too late for you to do anything about it now. Soon you will be completely helpless, and we'll exchange bodies." She shimmied her thin, bony shoulders. "Do you think you'll dare to show up at Planet Bang in this body? Will the boys still like you if you look like their great-grandmother?"

Serena stared at her, stunned. Even Jimena was unable to speak.

The woman held out her hand for the keys, her protruding cheekbones looking like those of a skeleton. "So now if you don't have any more questions, I'm tired and want to go home."

Someone rapped on the side of the car. The security guard from Planet Bang leaned in through the broken window. "What's going on?" he asked.

"Nothing." Jimena climbed out, eyes defiant, and slammed the car door.

The woman smiled up at the guard and absently brushed a few pebbles of broken glass aside. "I just drove by to remind my granddaughters that they have to be home by ten."

The security guard looked at the woman, his expression showing her that he didn't believe her, then he turned and went back to his post in front of the club.

Serena surrendered the keys.

The woman clasped them. "Soon I won't need to follow you. I'll be so strong inside you that I'll know everything you do. I'll be able to come and go as I please until—" She snapped her knobby fingers. "I'm you and you're me."

Serena crawled from the car, her knees so shaky, she didn't think she'd be able to stand. Jimena put a comforting arm around her.

"Don't worry. We'll stop her. There has to be a way."

The car jerked forward, easing into traffic.

Vanessa, Catty, and Tianna ran across the street and joined them.

"What happened?" Catty asked.

"The woman from the alley," Serena said softly. "She's taking over my body. . . . The headaches . . . dizziness . . ." Her words drifted away.

"Did you find out who she is?" Catty asked, frantic. "Maybe we can still do something . . . go back in time . . . something!"

Serena shook her head.

"You should have taken her car registration." Vanessa looked after the car. "Then we'd at least have her name."

"Too late now," Serena said, feeling defeated.

"It's never too late," Tianna said with confidence, her eyes narrowing in concentration as she pushed out with her telekinetic power to the fast-moving car.

At the corner the Lexus slowed, then

hitched, its frame seeming to shudder as it came to a stop in the middle of the street. The back tires spun, peeling off a layer of rubber and churning blue smoke into the air.

"We should have used Tianna in the first place," Jimena said to Serena as they ran toward the car.

"Don't lie to me," Serena answered, breathless. "I know you wanted to see if you could still jack a car. I can read your mind. Remember?"

Jimena smiled sheepishly.

When they reached the Lexus, Serena jerked open the passenger side door, shot her hand inside, snapped open the glove compartment, and rifled through the papers.

The woman jammed her foot on the accelerator. The engine revved, dashboard shimmering, but the car still didn't move.

The smells of exhaust and burned rubber became so strong that Serena could barely breathe. At last she found the car registration slip, took it out, and flicked it at the woman, and for the first time she saw fear in the woman's eyes.

"I know who you are now," Serena warned. She kept the paper and slammed the car door.

Immediately Tianna released her hold and the Lexus jerked forward, skidding at an awkward angle toward oncoming cars. Horns blared. The Lexus swerved back into its lane and blasted away.

Serena took deep breaths, willing her heart to find its natural rhythm again. She glanced at Jimena, wondering how she had survived living a life where things like this were everyday.

"That's why they call it *la vida loca*," Jimena said, seeming to understand, and took the car registration paper from Serena.

"Aura Triton," Vanessa read over her shoulder.

"Let's go over to my house," Catty suggested. "And search for her name on the Internet."

"Good idea," Tianna agreed, her eyes looking exhausted and bloodshot from the strain of using her power.

Serena cast a nervous glance over her shoulder and began walking with them, knowing that somewhere inside her, the woman was growing like a parasite.

CHAPTER FOURTEEN

FOG WAS ROLLING in by the time they reached Catty's house. Catty unlocked the front door, and they headed for the kitchen. While they were fixing something to eat, Serena sat at the computer in a small alcove near the dining room. Jimena brought in a chair and joined her, sipping a Pepsi.

"Ready?" Serena asked, and took in a deep breath, her fingers striking the keyboard. *Aura Triton* appeared on the screen, and she pressed ENTER.

The computer made a crackling sound, and the search came up with 133 entries.

Tianna, Catty, and Vanessa gathered behind her, reading over her shoulder.

"Look," Catty said incredulously, pointing. "'Aura Triton and mental illness.'"

"Open it," Tianna coaxed.

Serena's fingers trembled as she clicked the mouse.

The site opened and a stunning picture of Aura, taken in the 1950s, stared back at them.

"She was beautiful," Vanessa said, then read the caption below the photo. "'Aura Triton was a starlet in the 1950s, originally named Ann Anderson. Ann appeared in secondary roles in thirty-three films. In 1956 she complained that another person had possessed her body. Her delusion became so acute that her parents had her hospitalized. After she was discharged from the sanitarium, she changed her name to Aura Triton.'"

Serena stared at the screen in disbelief.

"Try Ann Anderson," Tianna suggested. "See what that brings up."

Serena used the tool bar to go back to search. She typed in *Ann Anderson,* and an impossibly long list appeared. She opened the first site in the *Variety* archives. An article talked about the tragic mental illness of a promising actress. Her eyes froze on the quote from Ann Anderson's father. He claimed that it felt as if his daughter had turned into a stranger.

"This is really creepy," Tianna said. "It sounds like she really was possessed by someone else."

Serena opened the next site. An old page from the *Los Angeles Herald-Examiner* came into focus on the screen. The headline read WOMAN IN HOSPITAL CLAIMS SHE IS THE REAL ANN ANDERSON. A nurse was quoted as saying that her eighty-year-old patient claimed she was the starlet Ann Anderson, trapped inside the invalid body of Aura Triton. The nurse found it odd that the movie actress Ann Anderson had changed her name to Aura Triton at the same time that her patient, also named Aura Triton, had insisted that she was the real Ann Anderson. She had called the

LAPD, but the detective had refused to take the case, saying that the idea was crazy. The nurse wasn't convinced.

Two hours later they had scanned through all the sites. Serena's eyes felt dry and tired.

"Do you think it's possible for a person to live forever by skipping from one body to the next?" Vanessa whispered.

"I think it is," Serena said in a jagged voice. "I know it is. I don't feel her presence all the time, but when she's there, I can tell. Usually it starts with a headache."

"Maybe my mother could help us," Catty said. "She knows about this stuff."

As if she had some psychic ability of her own, Kendra walked through the alcove on her way to the kitchen. "I thought you'd still be at Planet Bang. Are you working on a class project?"

They turned and stared at her.

"What?" Kendra asked.

"Mom," Catty said. "We need your help."

* * *

Kendra sat at the kitchen table, sipping ginger tea and listening patiently as they told her everything.

"I know it seems impossible to believe," Serena finished.

"No," Kendra answered, setting down her cup. "I believe you. In fact, I have a confession to make. At the psychic bazaar when I read your fortune, what I had actually seen in your coffee cup was *an enemy dwells within you.* That didn't make sense to me, so I changed it to *an enemy has come to visit.* Then I decided not to tell you what I had seen because I assumed that I had made a mistake in my reading."

Serena stared at her.

"So you'll help us?" Jimena asked.

Kendra nodded. "Let me do some research on the transmigration of souls from one living body to the next."

"I didn't even know such things existed." Tianna looked surprised.

Serena rubbed her forehead, wishing there were something she could do before the woman completely took over her psyche.

"Come on," Jimena ordered, standing. "It's late. I'll give everyone a ride home."

As they were walking down the street to the car, Serena became aware of Jimena, Vanessa, and Tianna arguing in gruff whispers behind her.

"What?" she asked, perplexed.

"We think you should ask Stanton for help," Vanessa said.

"Right," Serena answered sarcastically.

"Maggie is gone," Jimena added. "Kendra will take a few days researching, and we don't know how much time we have left."

"I can't believe you'd think Stanton could be the answer," Serena snapped. "You always hated it before when I would ask him for advice, and now you want him to help us."

"I think we need to talk to him," Jimena stated.

"He might know something," Vanessa added.

"No," Serena answered, but as she started to turn, she caught a furtive flicker in the shadows near the redwood fence and paused.

The night seemed to change then, as if something more than a breeze were skating through the air. An unnatural shadow wrapped around the oleander bush, its movement slow and easy. Serena's heart began to race. She took a quick step back and glanced at her amulet. It cast a rainbow of shimmering lights into the dark, warning her of a Follower's approach, but where was her goddess power? Her nerves should be thrumming, energy surging through her and preparing her for battle. But nothing was happening.

"What is it?" Tianna asked, her eyes wary, the glow of her amulet streaking into the shadows as if something portentous were about to happen.

"Let's get in the car and leave," Serena ordered in a low voice, but none of them moved. She didn't think she could bear looking into Stanton's eyes now that he had returned to the Atrox.

A darkness more solid than the other shadows slid toward her, wrapping around her before flitting away.

"There," Tianna whispered, pointing.

The night filled with a crackling sound, and

a figure poured from a rip in the air, inches from Serena. The small hairs on the back of her neck rose as if sensing his evil aura. The amulet thrummed against her chest, warning her to run, but she didn't move.

And then Stanton stood before her, his hair spiked and blond, the shaggy bangs hanging in his dangerous eyes.

Tianna sucked in a long draw of air and stepped closer to Serena. "I've never seen a shape changer before," she whispered.

Serena stared at Stanton, her body filling with old longing and new anxiety. Had he always been nearby, watching over her? Or was his visit one more in a long line of deceptions?

CHAPTER FIFTEEN

ERENA STARED INTO Stanton's blue eyes, breathing the familiar night air scent of him. She took a quick step back, not understanding her chaotic emotions or her disturbing physical attraction to him. She was a Daughter of the Moon, and Stanton was her enemy.

His hand reached up to touch her cheek, but she batted it away before he could.

"You summoned me, Serena, and now you're backing off," he said, his eyes looking at her with the gentleness she remembered.

"I didn't call you," she answered, feeling miserable and happy in the same moment.

"She needs your help," Jimena interrupted.

"Serena." He repeated her name longingly.

"No, I don't." Serena spoke with more anger than she had intended. She could feel the icy spirit of the Atrox surging through him. His evil pulsed in the air. Couldn't the others feel it? She hated him for what he had become, but other, familiar emotions were returning, and she didn't want him to see her pain.

"I'm sorry," he said softly.

Her head jerked back, studying him. Had he caught her sadness before she had even been able to hide it? Maybe it was impossible to conceal anything from him now.

Her moon amulet cast a ghostly light across his face, but it didn't seem to bother him. He cocked an eyebrow and tried to ease into her mind as he had done so many times before, but she stopped him and refused to listen.

"I can't trust you anymore," she said.

A flicker of hurt crossed his eyes, but she

knew that had to be an illusion. A person without a soul couldn't feel such emotion.

"You have the power to look in my mind," he said. "If you do, you'll know."

She watched him, not sure what she should do.

"I'm waiting." He stepped closer, his mind completely open to her.

She could feel the heat radiating from his body and took a deep breath, ignoring her aching need to embrace him. He had freely chosen to return to the Atrox. He was her enemy now.

"I haven't done anything to make you distrust me," he said.

"Maybe you can tell us what to do," Vanessa interrupted. She and Jimena quickly told Stanton everything they knew about Aura Triton. He listened quietly, and when they finished, he spoke.

"This is my fault," he said, almost to himself.

She stared at him in stunned silence.

"Aura loves Lambert," Stanton explained. "After I imprisoned him in my memories, it was only natural that she would retaliate by hurting the one person I love."

Serena's breath caught. Did Stanton still love her? How could he? She couldn't believe him anymore.

"I'm telling you the truth," he insisted, as if he had read her doubts.

"How can we stop Aura?" Jimena asked.

Stanton shook his head hopelessly. "I don't know of any way."

Serena gazed into his eyes and steadied her voice. "Next time we meet as enemies."

He stared at her, eyes desperately sad. "The only person I love is now my enemy."

She forced herself to nod and turn away from him.

He leaned back, blending with the darkness, and became a black mist, hissing into the air.

She blinked, trying not to think of him, but she couldn't forget the defeated look on his face.

CHAPTER SIXTEEN

F

RIDAY AFTERNOON, Serena rummaged
through her messenger bag outside Mrs.
Graham's language arts class. She had tucked
three new poems into the zippered side pocket,
and now the pages had been replaced with red lip
tint, green eye shadow, silver eyeliner, and oil-
blotting sheets. She leaned back, knocking her
head against the wall in total frustration, then
stared at her long red fingernails. She didn't
remember putting on the acrylic tips, but since
Tuesday the blackout periods had been increasing,
and always she came out of them resembling a

throwback to the 1950s. She was just glad that so far Aura hadn't cut her hair into one of those skull-hugging poodle styles she'd seen in her grandmother's photo albums.

Kids started to file into the classroom, most of them staring at her. She dreaded looking into a mirror. She could only imagine what Aura had done to her face this time. She glanced down at her watch and calculated the hours. She remembered leaving for school, but after that she was clueless as to what had happened until now.

She had started to follow the others inside when Vanessa grabbed her arm and yanked her back.

"What?"

"Catty wants us to cut class and meet at her house." Vanessa's large blue eyes looked up and down the hallway as if she expected a platoon of officers to descend upon them. She wrapped her brown sweater-coat tightly around her.

"Don't be so nervous." Serena tried to calm her. "I'll get us out of school."

Vanessa raked her fingers through her hair.

"I hate cutting classes. I'm only doing it now because we're running out of time." She looked at Serena curiously, then searched in her purse. "Here." She handed her a wad of Kleenex and a mirror. "Looks like Aura took you for a ride again. She's got some cheesy taste."

"Come on." Serena started walking, holding the mirror in front of her. She wet the tissue with the tip of her tongue and started rubbing at the thick black eyeliner that swept out from her eyes into wings.

Within twenty minutes they stood on Catty's porch, a late afternoon breeze stirring the wind chimes hanging from the eaves.

Jimena opened the door, her mood somber. "You weren't at school this morning." Her voice sounded angry, but Serena knew that Jimena turned her fears into anger as a way to cope.

They followed Jimena inside and up the stairs. Soothing guitar music played from the sound system in the living room.

Catty had repainted the walls in her

bedroom a shocking pink and trimmed the floor-boards and window ledges sherbet orange. The curtains and bedspread were now stark white. An easel stood in the corner. Sketch pads and pencils covered her desk, and canvases leaned against the walls. Serena glanced at the drawings scattered on the worktable in front of Catty. They looked like before and after Aura pictures of herself.

"Hey," Tianna greeted her. She sat in the but-terfly chair next to the bed, a zigzag part in her hair. "I'm glad you made it back."

"Me too," Serena answered. "I hope Kendra found something."

Catty stood. "Now that we're all here, let's go see what Mom's uncovered."

In the hallway Serena followed the others, her steps slow and hesitant. She wasn't sure she was ready to hear what Kendra had found. She gripped the banister, fearing that it might be bad news, then hurried down the stairs, crossed the living room, and stopped at the entrance to the kitchen, suddenly aware of how nervous she felt.

Kendra sat at the table, an array of papers

and books spread in front of her. Thin bluish smoke curled from a stick of sandalwood incense near her left hand.

They joined her, scooting chairs up to the table, and waited in silence.

At last Kendra looked up. "I have an answer—or part of it."

Serena gripped the side of her chair, waiting.

Kendra held up a steno pad. Penciled notes were jotted across the lines. "I found something in one of the manuscripts that Professor Hendrix gave me to translate. I was actually doing research on Circe for him."

"Who's Circe?" Serena asked.

"She was an ancient enchantress celebrated for her magic and knowledge of poisons. According to Homer, she gave men potions that changed them into beasts. Professor Hendrix thought her concoctions could actually be medicinal, and he wanted to see if we could find any of the formulas that might have been handed down and recorded by monks during the Middle Ages."

"You found something about Aura in that?" Tianna asked, looking surprised.

"I was going through a stack of manuscripts and the word *Aura* caught my eye. I'm not completely sure how this is related to Circe yet, but I translated the story about a young woman named Ursula. Her beauty was so renowned that knights leaving on crusades would stop by her father's hut just to look at her. They believed good fortune would befall them if they gazed into her eyes."

"What time period is that?" Serena asked.

"The thirteenth century."

"That's about the time Stanton was kidnapped by the Atrox," Vanessa said softly.

Kendra nodded and waited a moment before she went on, her finger running along the words written on the page. "According to the manuscript, the devil also saw her beauty and pursued her, offering her great wealth if she would betroth him. Knowing her father's poverty, she decided to sacrifice her life for the good of her family. She asked for only one gift for herself—"

"To preserve her beauty for eternity," Jimena interrupted.

Kendra smiled. "That's right. Apparently she suffered from vanity."

"But could Ursula be Aura?" Catty seemed skeptical. "That would mean she's been alive for centuries."

"There's more," Kendra continued. "Ursula betrayed the devil by falling in love with a mortal."

"Lambert." Serena gasped.

"The manuscript didn't give a name, but the devil found out and punished Ursula by destroying her beauty. She remained alive but in bodiless form and was called Aura after that."

"She's been alive for that long?" Tianna looked stunned.

Kendra nodded. "In Latin, *Aura* means the one who is like air. She lived as a wind spirit until she found a way to possess other bodies."

"Maybe she used a magic potion," Vanessa added. "One she got from Circe."

"The water," Serena said. "She gave me water to drink the first time I met her."

"I'm assuming that is the connection to Circe," Kendra agreed. "But so far I haven't found anything written about the elixir that Aura used or how she was able to possess another person. I'm on my way back to campus now to see if I can find out more."

After Kendra left, Serena took a deep breath. What she was thinking was dangerous, but she didn't see that she had a choice. "I think I have a plan to scare Aura into leaving my body."

"What?" Catty asked.

"She won't want a dead body," Serena whispered.

"What are you thinking, *chica*?" Jimena said sternly.

"It's risky," Serena explained. "But if Vanessa can make me invisible and keep me from falling, then I'm confident it will work."

"I'll do whatever you want me to do," Vanessa assured her.

"Then first we have to make a date with Aura," Serena said. "None of it will work unless she'll participate."

"You mean go see her?" Catty asked.

Serena nodded. "We have her address from the car registration."

An hour later they pulled into the wide circular drive on a hilltop estate in Malibu. The spiky shadows of palm fronds brushed across the sleek white facade. They crawled from the car and stared out at the peaceful waters of the Pacific Ocean.

"The view's incredible," Serena said, and started up to the front door.

"Go around to the back," Jimena said, motioning them onto a path of jet-black stepping-stones.

"Shouldn't we knock?" Vanessa asked.

"Follow her." Serena started after Jimena. "It's part of her power now; she just knows things."

They circled the house, passing long picture windows and marble statues, finally stepping onto a tiled patio. Aura was sitting in a lounge chair in a chartreuse swimsuit near the glittering waters of a vast pool. She lifted her oversized sunglasses and watched them walk toward her.

"Not long now," Aura said with amusement in her voice. She reached for a glass of ice water on the table next to her, her dark weathered skin hanging loose on her bones. "I like your nails, Serena. I can't wait to get into your body permanently."

Serena shuddered. If they couldn't get Aura to leave her mind, then eventually she would be trapped in a body that didn't look like it could survive another ten years.

Aura smiled as if she knew what Serena was feeling. "Did you bring your friends because you were hoping they could convince me to leave you?" She flipped the glasses back over her eyes. "Not likely."

Serena watched her own reflection in the black lenses.

"Well," Aura said at last. "You took all the trouble to find me. It must be important. Speak up."

"I want you to meet us out at the Palos

Verdes Peninsula tonight," Serena said, and handed Aura a paper with a map on it.

"So dramatic," Aura said. "Can't we discuss it over dinner at the Ivy? My treat."

"No," Serena answered.

"What have you done?" Aura asked. "Some kind of mumbo-jumbo charm?"

Serena shook her head.

"And what happens if I don't come?"

"I've made my decision," Serena stated flatly. "Now it's up to you."

"Oh, all right." Aura sighed heavily. "You young women always amuse me with your little plots."

Back in Jimena's car they sat silently, staring out at the ocean.

Finally Vanessa spoke. "There's something wrong. That was too easy."

"I know," Serena acknowledged, "but I can't read her mind. She blocks me, and all I pick up are my own thoughts."

Jimena started the car engine. "Maybe our plan is too dangerous."

"We just don't know enough about her yet," Tianna added. "Maybe if we waited—"

"Time isn't on our side," Serena interrupted.

"But if I took you back into the past to the day before you ran into her," Catty offered, "maybe we could change things." The air shimmered as if Catty were opening the tunnel she used to travel through time.

"That won't work. Remember? She's part of me now," Serena stated. "She'd only go back with us."

The air became still again.

"There must be a safer solution," Catty insisted. "This makes me nervous."

"I know, but we don't have a choice," Serena said firmly. "It's my last chance. Are you with me?"

With reluctance, they all agreed.

CHAPTER SEVENTEEN

Serena stared up at the starless night, her head resting against the car window as Jimena drove toward Rancho Palos Verdes. Catty, Vanessa, and Tianna sat still and quiet in the backseat, but Serena sensed their worry. The glow of city lights fell away as they rode through a neighborhood of Spanish-style villas, then turned onto another street with houses perched near sheer drops where the land had given way. The last home had been condemned as unsafe. Red paper warnings were stapled to the garage and front door.

"We're almost there," Jimena said, steering the car up a wide paved road that curved toward the point of the peninsula before winding back to San Pedro and the Port of Los Angeles. Bridle trails wound in and out of the trees.

A few minutes later they parked at the side of the road and climbed from the car. Serena breathed deeply, taking in the briny smell of ocean water.

Tianna switched on a small flashlight, and they followed the shaft of amber light over the dried grass to a small weathered fence marking the edge of the cliff. Some of the wood posts slanted at odd angles, the slats hanging free where the earth had caved into the ocean below.

"I'm going now," Vanessa whispered, her body already shimmering and taking on a strange speckled glow. She dissolved into a cloud that looked like a swarm of gnats and whirled away from them.

Serena took a deep breath. "Okay, I better

get ready. Stay back here. Just in case Aura has something else planned."

Jimena nodded, her eyes not letting any emotion through, but Serena eased into her mind and said good-bye.

"*Que vayas con Dios,*" Jimena whispered back.

Tianna flicked off her flashlight. "I'll use my power to make sure the land doesn't give way before you're ready."

"Thanks." Serena started walking.

"Good luck," Catty called after her.

Serena kicked off her shoes and stepped over the rickety fence, ignoring the glow-in-the-dark signs warning her to stay away from the unstable land. She inched to the edge of the cliff and curled her toes into the wet grass and dirt. The ocean wind lashed against her, tossing her hair wildly about. Sixty feet below, phosphorescent waves splashed over the jagged rocks, spraying sea foam into the night. She shuddered. She was terrified of heights.

The glare from car headlights brushed over her. She glanced back as the Lexus pulled onto the embankment, shooting straight at her. It stopped suddenly and parked in the grass. Aura stepped from the car, leaving the lights shining in Serena's eyes, and walked toward her, the end of her long yellow scarf twirling behind her.

"Is this what you're using to get me to leave?" she asked derisively. "You won't jump. You'd kill us both, not just me. Self-preservation is too dear to you."

"You're wrong." And without hesitation, Serena dove into the dark. Cold air raced around her at an unbelievable speed, stinging her face and leaving her breathless.

Aura's shrill scream pierced the night.

At the same moment Serena felt a racking pain as if something were boring through her head, and just when it became intolerable, the feeling left. It must have been Aura leaving her body.

"Success!" she shouted to Vanessa.

Immediately Vanessa's invisible form whisked around her, but Serena plunged through her.

Frantic, Vanessa swept around her again,

stringing her molecules into strands and trapping Serena in the webbing. This time Serena felt Vanessa's power working. Her skin began to prickle as her cells pulled apart.

But even with Vanessa's latticework beneath her, they were descending too fast. The ocean's cold slashed through Serena, tearing over muscle and bone. Becoming invisible had never hurt before. Suddenly her partially dissolved body snapped back together and she tumbled through Vanessa.

Vanessa gathered around her, trying to slow her tailspin, but Serena understood what was wrong now. They had forgotten to consider the speed of her fall. It made her too heavy for Vanessa to hold. And for her power to work, Vanessa needed to grasp Serena tightly against her.

A chill rushed through her. Serena had another problem. If Vanessa kept trying to catch her, the fall could kill them both. She sensed Vanessa's panic and refusal to give up.

"Let go," she yelled, kicking free.

Sea foam sprayed over her and she prayed, *"O Mater Luna, Regina nocis, adiuvo me nunc."*

CHAPTER EIGHTEEN

A VELVET DARKNESS swept around Serena, cradling her and carrying her out over the ocean. Her body began to fade, and then the night swallowed her.

"Stanton," she whispered with a start, enjoying despite herself the feel of his embrace, so tight and comforting around her. They soared aimlessly down the shore in silence, a shadow sliding over the breakers.

She knew she couldn't trust him, but her arms wrapped around him as if they had a will of their own, and when they materialized again on the rocky beach, she was still holding him. She looked into his blue eyes, visible in the dark, and caught a look of intense longing and desire. Why had she been so angry with him?

He traced a finger over her cheek. She flinched at first and pulled back but then he leaned forward, their lips inches apart, breath mingling and she didn't push him away. Finally he kissed her. She shivered.

Stanton swung her into his arms and carried her around piles of kelp, over the craggy rocks away from the breakwater, then set her down in the sand, his arm tight around her.

"I've missed you," she admitted at last, enjoying the phosphorescent beauty of the waves and the rhythmic roar of surf coming to shore.

"I know," he said as if he had always known her true feelings hidden under her distrust and anger. He cupped her face tenderly between his hands.

She closed her eyes and let him enter her mind, then he drew her back into his. The hypnotic trance feeling of being in his memories took over, and she relived what he had done during the time they had been separated, his remembrances now her own. She felt his anguish the night he had turned back to the Atrox and saw clearly that it had been the only way he could save her from Lambert. She shuddered, finally understanding the depth of the sacrifice he had made for her. As hard as the memory was to see, she knew living it had been immeasurably worse for him.

"Thank you," she whispered, overwhelmed, and knew at once that he had always been nearby, watching over her. Those dreamworld visits had not been illusions. He had come to her at night.

She didn't want to see anymore, but Stanton held her close and took her forward to the night he had walked into the Cold Fire for the second time. She felt awestruck again by the beauty of the frigid blaze and the crystalline patterns frosting over his arms and face from the lashing tongues of fire. She saw the ceremony through his eyes as members of the Inner Circle looked on, pleased that Stanton had destroyed the traitor Lambert. And even as the elders crowned him Prince of the Night, Stanton showed her that he had never lost his love for her. He had kept it hidden deep inside him.

When he was sure she had no lingering doubt about his devotion, he released her, and she was on the shore once again.

She smiled up at him, her hands moving around his waist, pulling him to her, but when his lips touched hers again, she felt something drawing her back into his mind. She thought at first that he had one last memory he wanted to show her, but without warning she was crashing through his thoughts at a reckless speed.

Memories blurred past her. She strained against the force, but she couldn't stop it. What was he doing to her? He had trapped Vanessa once in his memory of another time. Could he be imprisoning her the same way? Her heart fell. She had been deceived so easily.

Then Stanton yanked away from her as if the speed at which she was chasing through his mind had caused him a jolt of pain. She clutched his shoulders, terrified. If he wasn't doing this to her, then what was happening? She struggled desperately, trying to resist the force. She fought against it with her mental power, but it was stronger.

Her head throbbed with shards of pain as the strange energy sucked her deeper and deeper inside Stanton. The outside world fell away, and she knew she was lost inside him now. She began to shiver.

And then she felt Stanton warn her, *Aura is still inside you! She's doing this to you.*

Now she understood why Aura hadn't been reluctant to meet them at the peninsula. She had never wanted to possess Serena's body as a way to get revenge. She had always been waiting for an opportunity to use Serena's power to go inside Stanton's memories. She wanted to free Lambert.

Another presence joined her and she realized it was Aura, drawing her down. They plunged into horrific recollections. A whir of long-ago times flashed by Serena, yesterdays she was certain Stanton had never wanted her to see, centuries of his secret life spent turning innocents to the Atrox. Their despairing screams echoed around her, filling her with grief, as Aura continued bringing her deeper still.

The journey stopped abruptly in cold blackness, the faint scent of sulfur wafting in the air. Serena's eyes could not see in the dark, but she sensed something hovering around her. Her heart pounded as an ominous pressure slid closer to her with terrible ease.

Stanton had imprisoned Lambert in his memories of the Atrox. Was it here? The billowing darkness surged and grew, lashing around Serena with horrible compression until she felt engulfed by it and unable to breathe. Slowly she turned and stared into the face of the Atrox, abiding where Stanton's soul should be. Its raw hate made her tremble. Alarm shot through her. Had Aura made a bargain with the Atrox to take Lambert and leave Serena in his place?

CHAPTER NINETEEN

SUDDENLY A BLUE pulsing light appeared, casting a strange glow over the dark.

"Lambert," Serena whispered. Already she could feel his chilling power. All of the Daughters would be in danger if he were free. They had not been able to defeat him before, and she sensed that he had somehow become stronger while imprisoned inside Stanton.

"I've come for you." Aura's joy was immense. "I promised nothing would ever separate us."

With a wrench Serena and Aura were

speeding back over Stanton's life history, the blue light streaking with them. The pain inside Serena became unbearable now. Aura had consumed most of Serena's power in her haste to find Lambert, and the velocity of their escape was draining what little strength remained. But as exhausted as she felt, this was better than being left in Stanton's memory of the Atrox.

At last Serena was back on the beach in her mind and body again, breathing the salty air. Instantaneously Aura ripped from her with a savage jolt. Serena stumbled, hot pain surging through her, and fell to the sand, shaken, trying to clear her thoughts but thankful to be free from Aura's possession.

She glanced up at Stanton. He seemed to be in a trance, staring sightless into the night. She watched helplessly as a blue glow shimmered around him. She tried to summon her strength to fight Lambert, but Aura had depleted her power, and without her energy she had no way to protect even herself. Defeated, she waited to see what would happen next.

The haunting light cloaked Stanton, then gathered, rolling into a tight ball, and shot from him with an explosive force, flashing over the ocean like a flare. A luminous glow filled the night sky, colors shimmering from pale blue to deep green, finally shifting to violet.

Serena stood and took a shaky step forward, awestruck, marveling at the spectacle. Lambert was trying to create a fearful form to scare her, but instead the sky left her breathless with wonder.

"Stay close," Stanton cautioned, and pulled her back. Whatever spell he had been under was broken.

The light died at once and darkness pushed around them again. Serena listened, trying to fathom what might happen next, but all she could hear was the comforting rush of surf.

"It's my fault this happened," she said quietly. "I thought Aura had left me when I jumped off the cliff."

"I did, too," Stanton agreed. "It seemed that she had."

"I should have understood what she was

planning all along." Serena shook her arms, trying to release the tension building in her body.

"How could you?" Stanton asked. "No one has ever been able to release someone imprisoned in memory." But before she could answer, his finger touched her lips, cautioning her to be quiet, and then she felt what he must have been sensing.

A strange energy gathered around them. Her hair began to prickle as an electric charge accumulated in the air. She swiped her hand back and forth, feeling the unnatural fuzzy texture in the atmosphere. Tiny blue sparks crackled and shot off the tips of her fingers, discharging the buildup of static electricity.

"How is he doing this?" she asked.

"Lambert became stronger while he was imprisoned inside me," Stanton said, his eyes watchful as if he were anticipating something more.

"How?" Serena asked, wondering if Stanton had night vision now. She could only see the foaming waves and the electrified striations dancing around her hands.

The ocean breeze stopped suddenly as if the air had become too heavy to move.

"He found a way to drain my power," Stanton answered. "I couldn't stop him without setting him free."

"Why didn't you release him, then?" Serena was struggling to breathe now. The change didn't seem to be affecting Stanton.

"I knew he would hunt you down if I did," Stanton explained, his eyes searching the sky.

Without warning the sand along the beach swirled into an enormous cloud.

"What now?" Serena asked, her mouth dry with fear.

Electrical veins shot from the spinning sands, small at first but increasing in size until a jagged fork of lightning struck the side of the cliff, releasing the smell of ozone. Immediately the night exploded with thunder. Sparks burst from the impact of the strike, flying in circles before landing in the chaparral. A scrub oak caught fire and rolled down the side of the cliff to the tidepools, cinders falling in its wake.

Small fires bobbed in the tidal waters before going out.

The sandy wind shrieked at Serena, and she knew if she were caught in it, she wouldn't be able to breathe the gritty air, but she didn't have the strength to run or fight.

Stanton stood protectively in front of her, facing the swelling cloud, a primal vibration building inside him.

Serena felt the unholy power surging through him and knew at once that he was channeling the energy of the Atrox. It terrified her. Then spears of light stabbed the sky, piercing the surging sands. A booming concussion shook the beach and the cloud stopped. Sand rained across the shores, falling in massive dunes and hollows. Stillness followed.

"He's backed off for now," Stanton said, but there was too much caution in his voice, as if he sensed something more.

"Up there." Serena pointed.

The blue light swept up the rugged cliff to the silhouette of a thin woman.

"Aura has him now," Serena said. "Maybe they'll be satisfied to be together again and leave us alone." But even as she spoke, she could feel Stanton's doubt.

"*¡Oye, chica!*" Jimena's voice disrupted the quiet.

Serena turned. Catty, Tianna, Vanessa, and Jimena charged across the sand toward them, the beam from Tianna's flashlight guiding their way.

"Vanessa told us that a shadow saved you." Catty squeezed her. "I'm so glad you're okay. You can't imagine what we thought when Vanessa came back to us alone!"

"What was that glow in the sky?" Tianna asked.

"It was Lambert," Serena said.

"He's free?" Vanessa's eyes were wide with fear.

"What happened?" Jimena asked impatiently. Even in the dim light Serena could see the concern on her face.

"Aura never left my body when I fell," Serena told them.

"All that for nothing." Vanessa sighed.

"She must have known that I wouldn't let anything happen to Serena," Stanton said.

"She never wanted to possess my body in the way we thought," Serena explained. "She was waiting for a chance to use my power to go inside Stanton's mind."

"So she could free Lambert," Tianna finished.

"I think we should go," Jimena said, pointing back to the cliff.

"I want to get out of here, too." Vanessa started walking. "Something feels wrong."

They trudged over the sand to the rocks.

"How did Aura get involved with Lambert anyway?" Catty asked, stepping onto a wet outcropping.

The spray from the breakers crashed over them, and Serena slipped on a pile of spongy seaweed. Stanton caught her and settled his arm around her.

"Her beauty was legendary, so perfect that even the Atrox wanted her," Stanton said.

"Legend says she had agreed to betroth the devil, but it was really the Atrox."

Serena shuddered, remembering the foreboding black cloud in which the Atrox dwelled.

"Lambert didn't see her until the Atrox asked him to escort her to the underworld," Stanton went on. "But the moment Lambert saw her, he fell desperately in love with her. He knew the risk in defying the Atrox, but his love for Aura was stronger than his fear."

"I bet that's when he started plotting to overthrow the Atrox," Jimena said.

"Yes," Stanton continued. "Aura had assumed that the Atrox didn't know of her deception, so she eagerly stepped into the Cold Fire. But instead of giving her immortality, the flames reduced her body to ashes. She remained alive, but as a wind spirit. That's when people started calling her Aura."

"Why wasn't Lambert punished?" Tianna asked. The beam of her flashlight found a narrow footpath cut into the side of the cliff and she started up.

"The Atrox tried to force her to name her lover," Stanton said. "But she never revealed Lambert's identity."

"How did she get her first body?" Catty asked, catching herself as the edge of the footpath gave way beneath her. Pebbles tumbled down to the rocks.

"Lambert found an enchantress named Circe who was celebrated in ancient times for her skill in magic," Stanton said. "She concocted a potion."

"The water Aura made me drink." Serena remembered its bitter taste.

"Yes, and since then," Stanton went on, "Aura has been migrating from one body to the next for centuries, taking over the bodies of strong young women and forcing their souls into the aging one she abandons."

"But how do you know so much about it now when you didn't know anything about it before?" Jimena asked, skeptically.

"I knew that Aura loved Lambert," Stanton answered. "And that she might try to take Serena in retaliation, but I didn't think her skill would be great enough to possess a Daughter. When I realized it was, I tried to find answers."

"Why did she bring me back with her?" Serena asked, finally voicing the worry that had been troubling her. "I thought she was going to trade me for Lambert and leave me with the Atrox."

"She couldn't do that," Stanton explained. "It was your power that propelled her into my memories, and she needed it again in order to escape."

Serena turned back, sensing that Stanton had paused.

He stared up at the top of the cliff as if something made him wary. "Lambert gave up too easily."

Jimena stopped on the path ahead of Serena, her body tense. "What do you think he's got planned?"

Stanton shook his head, eyes focused on the ridge. "I don't know."

"Check it out," Jimena whispered.

Serena looked up, following her gaze.

Above them an orange glow filled the darkness. They paused, watching the eerie light become steadily brighter.

"What is it?" Vanessa asked in a haunted voice.

A Follower stepped to the edge of the cliff, holding a torch high in the air above him. Wind rushed around the flame, tossing it wildly. Then one by one others joined him, each holding a blaze, until a solid line blocked the path.

"The *infidi*," Stanton whispered.

Serena remembered the word tattooed on Tymmie's back and above the girls' hips in her dream.

"The Followers who are trying to overthrow the Atrox," Stanton said. "I won't let them succeed."

Serena's head whipped back, staring at Stanton. He loved her, but he was still loyal to the Atrox. The idea made her angry again.

"We can't fight so many." Serena felt doomed. "We can't even stand together to combine our powers. We'll fall over the ledge if we do."

The first Follower stepped down the path, the fire at the end of his pole lighting his way and making shadows stretch and twist over the side of the cliff to the rocks below.

Cold terror settled over Serena as the line of Followers descending the path grew long.

CHAPTER TWENTY

"THEY WANT ME," Stanton whispered, pulling Serena behind him, his eyes never leaving his enemy. "Take the path back down to the beach and find another way up."

"You need our help." Jimena stayed in front of him.

He ignored her and, balancing precariously on the edge of the trail, stepped around her.

Unexpectedly the Followers surged forward, charging down the path, their torches whipping in savage circles. The earth rumbled beneath their steps. Mud clods and pebbles gave way, pitching to the rocks below.

Stanton shoved in front of Tianna and Vanessa, then turned back. "This isn't your battle," he warned. "Go."

The look on his face terrified Serena.

"Stanton." She started to walk up to him, but a shower of dirt and sandstone stopped her. Whipping her hands up to protect her face, she lost her balance. She took a faltering step and teetered on the edge.

Tianna caught her around the waist and pulled her back. The flashlight fell, bounced once, then rolled over the rim, shattering on the rocks below.

"If they don't stop running soon, they're going to make an avalanche," Tianna said, studying the slope as if she were trying to find a place to use her telekinetic power to make the land hold.

"What do they care?" Jimena asked. "They're probably all Immortals."

Serena glanced down. Light from the fires reflected off the wet craggy rocks and frothing surf.

"Here we go!" Catty yelled.

Fissures broke across the grainy sediment, widening into zigzag cracks, then the earth gave way.

Serena crashed down the face of the cliff, dragging her hands over the eroded edges to slow her fall. Her feet caught on a jutting piece of stone. She pressed against the sandstone facade, her cheek tight against the gritty surface, breathing in dirt and dust.

Rocks continued to bounce over her, and then the ground seemed calm again.

"Jimena!" Serena moved her head, her hands burning with scrapes and cuts.

"I'm okay," Jimena called in a rasping voice. "I can see Vanessa and Tianna. They made it back to the path."

"Where's Catty?" Serena asked.

"Here," Catty called back.

Serena glanced down. Catty clutched the

edge of the shelf on which they stood, her fingers slipping. Serena leaned over, muscles straining, and with Jimena pulled her up to join them. Catty's added weight split the crag.

"Not again!" Catty looked down.

Helplessly Serena watched as the rift grew larger. "I don't think it's going to hold," she shouted, and pointed to a scrub oak growing from the side of the slope. "Jump!"

They lunged as the earth fell crumbling into the ocean.

Serena caught a shredded branch. The bark scratched into the cuts on her palms. She swung out her legs and caught another outcropping with the tip of her toe, then strained and dug her fingers into a rivulet eroded into the sandstone surface. She pulled herself over, then, gripping hard, spit sand and dirt from her mouth before starting down.

"Follow me," she yelled, breathless as more rocks tumbled over her.

She continued climbing downward until she found a wave-cut terrace that connected to the path. She inched across the slippery bank, making room for Jimena and Catty. Finally they joined her, perching dangerously together, waves crashing inches below them.

Serena strained and glanced up at Stanton. He stood stone still, waiting for the Followers to attack. "Why doesn't he do something?" she asked.

"I think he was waiting to make sure we got away," Jimena answered.

And then the air trembled with his power. Followers in the front hesitated as an ominous halo glowed around him.

"As Prince of Night he has the power to destroy even Immortals," Catty whispered.

Stanton released his force with deadly accuracy and speed, sending swift bolts of light in all directions. Sparks flew into the air, giving the illusion of stars crowding the universe.

The Followers stopped, stunned, as if they had not expected his strength to be so great.

Serena glanced up and saw the blue light, hovering near the edge of the cliff. "He can't fight them and Lambert, too," she said. "We need to help him."

"It's too late for that." Jimena pointed up.

Serena watched with horror as Stanton leaned into the air and faded into an ebony shadow.

Immediately Followers dove after him, dropping their torches and changing as they fell into phantom forms. Their sinister shapes stretched and soared out across the night until the sky was shrouded with strange ghostly figures.

Their torches spiraled down, bouncing against the side of the cliff and setting fires in the dry chaparral.

"They're all shape changers," Serena said with dismay, gazing at the odd apparitions chasing after Stanton's raven-black silhouette.

"How can there be so many?" Catty asked.

The specter shadows twisted together, forming a huge cloud, then twined around Stanton's dusky shape. A hellish roar of victory followed, the strident sound echoing across the shore.

"They caught him," Serena whispered, her heart skipping a beat. She understood that

Stanton had sacrificed himself again in order to save her. He would have had the power to fight them all if he hadn't kept Lambert imprisoned inside him, stealing his power.

Stanton's last thoughts wove into her mind. *I love you, Serena.* And then all sense of him was gone.

The inky cloud shot upward and disappeared.

CHAPTER TWENTY-ONE

FIRE RACED OVER the dried chaparral, filling the air with the pungent odors of burning sage and smoke. Serena was the last one up the trail. Embers and ash swirled around her as she stepped over the weathered fence at the top of the cliff. In the distance sirens blared.

"We better get out of here before the fire trucks come." Jimena started running. Serena jogged beside her. The others sprinted ahead.

"I have to help Stanton," Serena said to Jimena. "There's got to be something I can do."

"Save your energy for breathing." Jimena coughed, waving at the drifting smoke.

Flames shot into the sky, catching the tops of palm trees on the bluff. Fire exploded in the dry fronds with a loud whoosh, bathing the night in a red glow. Sparks cascaded over them as Jimena unlocked the car doors.

"Get in," Jimena ordered.

They slipped in, taking deep breaths of the clean air inside.

Jimena ran to the driver's side, yanked open the door, and jumped behind the steering wheel. She started the car, tugged the gearshift into drive and stomped her foot hard on the accelerator, then swung the car into a looping U-turn.

Minutes later a fire engine rumbled past them, the siren piercing the night, its lights strobing over them.

Serena stared at the soot-streaked faces of her friends in the back. "We have to find a way to help Stanton." Her chest felt heavy with grief.

"I don't think we should do anything," Catty said, grabbing a beach towel off the floor and rubbing it over her face. "It's their war."

"Remember when we tried to bring Stanton back?" Serena asked, her throat sore and dry.

"We thought he was dead," Vanessa said, taking the towel from Catty and running it through her hair. "But he had actually gone to the Dark Goddess."

Serena nodded. "She warned Stanton that a war in the underworld could create repercussions in the world of light. If we don't do something, innocent people could be harmed."

"But how are we going to stop them?" Catty asked hoarsely. "You saw what they can do. We can't fight a swarm of shadows. We wouldn't even know which way to send our power."

"I'm starved," Tianna interrupted, passing the towel up to Serena. "I need something to clear my throat. Stop at the Wienerschnitzel so we can get some hot dogs."

"How can you think about eating?" Vanessa snapped.

"I'm hungry, too," Catty answered, digging into her pocket for money. "I can't believe you don't want something to drink. My throat's killing me."

"*Tengo hambre también.*" Jimena turned into the Wienerschnitzel drive thru, and minutes later they sat in the parking lot, bags of chili-cheese dogs with sauerkraut and pickles on their laps, giant paper cups of Pepsi in their hands.

The night guardsman walked past the car, eyeing them suspiciously.

Jimena took a long swallow of Pepsi, then turned to Serena as she unwrapped a steaming bun. "Remember when I used my power to see the future? I thought I had pictured you and Stanton fighting side by side against Followers who wanted to overthrow the Atrox."

"But I didn't fight with him," Serena said, wiping chili off her hand.

"I know, but some of what I saw in my vision matched what happened tonight," Jimena went on. "I only misinterpreted it. But now I know I was seeing the future—it wasn't my imagination playing tricks on me." She paused and added, "I never told you the second part."

Serena glanced at her, apprehension growing. "What else did you see?"

"I saw you leaving us and choosing to remain with Stanton," Jimena said, her black eyes solemn.

Serena shook her head. "That will never happen. Besides, you just said that you were wrong about the way you had interpreted the last vision, so maybe you're wrong about the second part, too."

Jimena didn't look convinced.

"I understand the danger." Serena felt miserable. How could she not help Stanton after he had risked so much to help her? "But Stanton risked his soul to save me. Don't I have to do the same for him?"

"You might be risking more than he did," Jimena argued.

Vanessa leaned forward, her blue eyes huge as if she were becoming exasperated with Serena's stubbornness. "Can't you see that this could still be a trick?"

"Then why didn't they destroy us when we were hanging from the cliff?" Serena turned and stared at Vanessa. "We were totally vulnerable then."

"Vanessa's right," Catty said.

"How?" Serena asked, her voice rising in frustration.

"You've forgotten that you're the one Lambert wanted in the first place. He needs you to overthrow the Atrox because you're the key," Catty responded.

Serena flinched.

"Maybe while Lambert was imprisoned inside Stanton," Tianna said thoughtfully. "They came to some kind of understanding and decided to work together."

"They hate each other," Serena answered with confidence. "Besides, I was inside Stanton, too. I know his thoughts."

"It wouldn't be the first time enemies joined forces," Vanessa pointed out.

"They're setting us up," Jimena said.

"How can you be so sure?" Serena asked.

Jimena took a last bite of hot dog and swallowed before speaking. "Aura agreed to meet us too easily, and it was a trap. Now Stanton is captured, and we don't even know it's real. All we saw were whirling shadows. It could all be part of the same plan."

"He's deceived us before," Catty added.

"He isn't setting a trap," Serena argued.

"How do you know?" Vanessa asked softly. "As Prince of Night, he has the power to destroy Immortals, yet he didn't. He let them catch him."

"He was trying to get them away from us so we'd be safe," Serena insisted.

Jimena wiped her hands on a paper napkin, then looked at Serena. "Maybe he wanted it to look that way."

Serena turned and stared out the window. "I have to take the chance. I can't be concerned for my own safety when someone needs my help."

"This isn't just someone," Jimena reminded her. "It's Stanton. The next in line to the throne of the Atrox."

"Let's at least hear her plan," Tianna suggested,

gathering up the wrappers and cups for the trash bin. "I hate Followers more than any of you, but I think we should listen to what Serena has in mind."

"When Aura had control over my body, she went partying," Serena started. "I saw where these new Followers hang out. I can go there and pretend that Aura is still in control of my body. I'll find out what's happening and see for myself if Stanton is part of a trap or if he needs rescuing."

"It's too dangerous," Catty said. "Lambert will be with the real Aura. The Followers will know you're not possessed by her."

"Besides, it's the dark of the moon tomorrow night," Vanessa pointed out. "Followers are most powerful then, and we'll be at our weakest."

Serena stared out the side window at the sliver of moon hanging in the smoky sky. "I'll go tonight, then."

"Aura used up all your energy freeing Lambert," Jimena reminded her. "Without your power, you won't even be able to communicate with us and tell us if you're in trouble."

Serena clutched her moon amulet and felt an

immediate comfort. Maggie had told her that she would always know intuitively what to do. She cleared her mind of all their arguments and a serenity came over her.

"I have to do it," Serena answered. "I have no choice. Besides, I know it's not a trap."

"Ya vas a ver," Jimena said with annoyance. "You'll see."

"If you go, you'll go alone," Vanessa said quietly from the back. "It's too risky."

The others agreed.

Serena nodded, disheartened, and they started home.

CHAPTER TWENTY-TWO

THE COMFORTING smells of Pop-Tarts and hot cocoa greeted Serena when she walked into the warm kitchen. Collin sat in a chair, legs propped on the oak table, a thick textbook in his lap, his attention focused on the TV in the corner on the counter.

"Hey." He turned his head. She could see from his expression how worried he'd been about her.

She stared at the small screen. The news video showed police helicopters circling over the fire on the cliffs at the Palos Verdes Peninsula while Coast Guard boats patrolled the ocean past the breakers, their floodlights scanning the waves. Fire trucks were parked on the street above, fire-fighters rolling out their hoses. The raging flames twisted into a hellish maelstrom, casting embers and sparks across the night.

Collin swung his feet down to the floor, snapped his book shut, and stood. "Where's Jimena?" he asked, hitching up his blue sweat-pants.

"She's okay. We were just in a fight." Serena washed her hands in the sink, then splashed water on her face. She took a paper towel, wet it, and cleaned the back of her neck.

"There was a report about teens with illegal firecrackers starting the fire." He motioned with his thumb at the breaking news on the screen.

"Followers," she said dryly, and poured simmering milk from the pan on the stove into a yellow mug, then added heaping teaspoons of cocoa.

"They took Stanton. I've got to help him, and the others are telling me it's a trap."

"Stanton?" Collin didn't bother to hide his surprise. "I thought you hated him now."

Serena walked over to the TV and turned it off with a click. "I was wrong," she said, and slumped into a chair, stirring her hot chocolate.

Collin sat down facing her, then leaned forward, his elbows resting on the table. "Tell me."

She sighed and recounted what had happened. When she had finished telling him everything, she added, "I can't abandon Stanton. Not after everything he's sacrificed for me."

Collin didn't hesitate. "Then do it. If you step back from what you know is the right thing to do, then you'll live the rest of your life scared—and I'm not talking about that haunted-house kind. I mean the kind that keeps you from being you."

Serena nodded. She understood Collin's philosophy, but that didn't stop the fear galloping through her right now. She didn't know if she was brave enough to do what was needed.

"Do you have a plan?" He interrupted her thoughts.

"I do," she confessed. "But I'm really, truly afraid."

He smiled at her.

"That's not exactly the response I was expecting." Serena stared at him. Why did he seem happy?

"I have something for you," he said, pushing back his chair with a loud scrape.

"What?"

"I'll show you. Wait here. I'll be right back."

Collin ran from the kitchen, his footsteps thundering up the stairs. In a few minutes he came back and handed her a gold orb with a sapphire set in the middle, hanging on a leather necklace. "Here."

"This is for me?" Serena asked, mesmerized by the beauty of the gem.

"Take it." He placed it around her neck. "I had forgotten about it, but when I was going through my closet this afternoon looking for some old photos to show Jimena, I found it."

When the dark blue jewel touched her, it quivered, thrumming against her chest as if something ancient and magical had been awakened inside it. At once she felt her goddess power surging inside her. Her breath caught as an odd tingling rolled through her.

"My power is back," she whispered.

Collin smiled at her.

Serena stared at the orb. "Where did you get it?"

"One of our baby-sitters gave it to me years ago," he explained. "She told me that one day you could need it and I would know when."

"Which one was she?" Serena asked. "We must have had twenty or more different baby-sitters when we were kids."

"You can't have forgotten her," Collin insisted. "She always wore these keys around her neck, hanging from thick chains, and when she walked, they made a rattling sound. You thought the clatter came from her bones."

Serena shook her head. "I can't remember her."

"Sure, you must; you loved her so much. She was a strange old lady. Her brown eyes looked milky as if she were blind, but she saw everything."

"What happened to her?" Serena asked.

"Dad fired her because of her dogs. He told her, no animals, but she always brought those old hounds with her. They made a disaster in the backyard and the neighbors complained about the dogs howling at night. You don't remember that?"

"I don't need to," Serena said. "I know who she is."

Collin looked at her curiously.

"The dark goddess Hekate," she whispered.

"Hekate?" Collin repeated. "You can't mean her."

"The charm," Serena explained, holding it up. "It's Hekate's circle."

Collin looked worried. "You mean the goddess who guides people in and out of Hades?"

"Yes."

He opened his Greek mythology text and thumbed through the pages. "Here." His finger ran across the words. "'Hekate was thought to cause nightmares. The earliest reliable records show her sending ghosts.'" He skipped down the page and continued. "'In later literature, the restless dead and the spirits of dogs wandered with her. The sound of barking dogs always preceded her appearance—'" He looked up at Serena. "Are you sure?"

Serena nodded. "She's also known for her skills in divining and foretelling the future. She must have seen the problem I'm having now."

A look of awe came over Collin's face. "Can you trust her?"

"Yes." Serena lifted the sphere. "Hekate is often misunderstood now, but once she was considered a powerful force of good." She paused and added, "She guided Jimena back from death after Jimena risked her life saving me from the Atrox."

Collin looked stunned, but no longer disbelieving.

Serena examined the amulet. "There's an engraving in Latin on the back," she said. "It has to be a message from Hekate."

"Read it." Collin's excitement seemed to match her own.

"*Leva velamen*," she said. "Lift the veil."

"What do you think it means?"

She shook her head. "I don't know yet." Then she glanced at the clock. It was only a little after ten. There was still time. "I better get ready."

"You're going to go without the others?" Collin asked.

She nodded. "That's where I'm meant to be."

She showered quickly, then stared in her closet, trying to decide what Aura would choose to wear. She had to be convincing. Her life depended on it.

Finally she slithered into a slinky blue micro-mini and a daring halter top. She loved the luxurious feel of the silk against her skin. Then she applied dusty eye shadow over her eyelids out to her temples, trying to recall how Aura had drawn the catlike provocative lines. When that was done, she coated her lashes with mascara and filed the jagged edges of her dragon nails.

At last she stared at her reflection. She liked

her wicked look. She sprayed Joy perfume over her body, slipped into spiky sandals, and went downstairs.

When she walked into the kitchen, Collin looked up. An involuntary whistle escaped his lips, and then a slow smile crossed his face. "Man, do you look different."

"I'm trying to look . . ." She thought a moment. "Less goddess and more . . . evil."

"You've succeeded." His eyes said it all.

She grabbed a coat and slipped it on. No way was she riding a bus in what she wore. She started to leave.

"Serena," Collin called after her.

She turned back.

"Don't you want me to give you a ride?" he asked.

She shook her head. "No, thanks."

"Be careful."

"I always am."

"I just have this funny feeling," he said, and kissed her lightly on the cheek.

"No fear," she whispered.

"No fear," he repeated, and she walked out the door.

When she stepped out to the street, she saw Jimena's Oldsmobile parked at the curb. Jimena sat on the hood in fluorescent blue leather jeans, a silky top, and strappy sandals. Her black hair was still wet from a shower.

Serena joined her at the car. Catty, Vanessa, and Tianna were waiting in the back, clean now and wearing velvet spaghetti-strap halters with bare backs. They looked ready to party.

"No way were we going to desert you," Jimena said, opening the car door.

Serena stopped and hugged her before getting inside. The interior still smelled of smoke.

"If you go down, then we all do," Tianna assured her.

"We won't be able to go inside the club with you," Vanessa explained. "The Followers will never believe that Aura is in your body if you show up with us, but as soon as you free Stanton, we'll be ready to fight the Followers."

"The only problem is how you're going to

tell us," Jimena said.

"I got my power back," Serena said, grateful to have such loyal friends.

"What happened to your look?" Catty teased.

"Yeah," Tianna agreed. "You look like your demonic twin."

Serena sighed. "I tried to imitate Aura's style."

They laughed nervously, and now that Serena had her power back, she could feel how worried they really were.

"Where to?" Jimena asked.

"The City of Commerce," Serena answered.

Twenty minutes later the car buzzed down an off-ramp and crept into a vast warehouse district near the freight rail yard. Many of the old factories and warehouses had been restored and converted into stores and office spaces, but others were still abandoned.

"There." Serena pointed. Weeds clung to the high mesh fence circling an old factory. Trash was caught in the coils of razor wire at the top. "Turn down that corner."

"Someone busted out all the streetlights," Jimena whispered.

A strange heavy feeling settled on Serena as the car headlights shone over the railroad tracks.

"It's here," she whispered. "I remember the tracks from my dream."

Jimena pulled to the side of the road and shut off the lights. The darkness was complete now and filled with an eerie tension.

Serena opened the car door.

Jimena turned to her. "*Ten cuidado.* Be careful."

Serena nodded and hoped she wasn't bringing her friends to their death.

CHAPTER TWENTY-THREE

SERENA CROSSED OVER the railroad tracks, her sandals crunching in gravel, and headed up the cracked concrete slab to an abandoned factory. Techno music vibrated through the rust-stained corrugated walls, and light shimmered from the glazed dormer windows in the roof. When she reached the weathered door, her skin prickled as if sensing the evil energy inside. She took a deep breath and went in.

She waited for her eyes to adjust to the gloomy light coming from three bare bulbs hanging near the dirt-streaked skylights. The interior was hot and steamy, reeking with cigarette smoke. The foul odors of petroleum distillates still hung in the air, left over from when the vast room had been used for manufacturing.

"No fear," she whispered to herself, then she tossed back her hair and let her body find the beat. She danced through the cables hanging in the entry and slid into the frenzy of moving arms and feet.

Her hips gyrated with strangers in time to the hectic tempo. She looked around the room with a bold stare and an audacious grin. No one seemed to wonder what a Daughter of the Moon was doing at their party. Then she remembered she had dressed like a demon tonight, not a moon goddess.

She studied the Followers dancing with her. Girls wore frosty eye shadows, the shimmering blues and pinks streaming over their eyelids into their temples and streaking into their hair. Their tight stomachs were bare, and each daredevil roll of their bodies showed off the curling INFIDUS tattoos below their waists.

"Let's dance." A guy rocking next to her grabbed her arm and pressed her against him, obvious desire on his sweating face.

She yanked away, but another Follower brushed an uninvited hand over her bare back. Silver barbells pierced his eyebrows and the bridge of his nose. His black jeans were tucked into black biker boots, and studded leather cuffs circled his wrists. His eyes looked at her as if he were eager to do something more than dance. She gave him a sultry smile and eased away.

The DJ music stopped, and a guy with waist-length hair ran across a catwalk suspended from the ceiling. He grabbed a microphone. Red leather cuffs covered his arms from wrists to elbows, and his short-sleeved tee was ragged and torn, his jeans shredded, revealing dark, muscular legs.

"Test. Test!" The microphone screeched, making everyone grab their ears. He smiled as if he had done it on purpose, then picked up his guitar and began to play. Metallic notes ripped through the air.

The overhead lights went out and a drummer pounded a wild jungle beat. The strobe light began pulsing at a slow pace that left ghostly images dancing in the dark following the flashes.

During one of the light flares Serena caught a glimpse of Jerome. He was an Initiate now, no doubt about that, but she wondered why an Initiate would be involved with Followers planning to overthrow the Atrox.

She threaded through the dancers to where she had seen him.

In the next burst of light his face seemed skeletal and wan. She wondered if they had taken him against his will or if he had been eager to join the dark side. His eyes met hers during a blast of light and she saw suspicion in his gaze. Had he already detected her charade? But instead of backing away from him, she let a slow, easy smile glide over her face.

"I'm glad you're here," he said at last. "I was afraid you weren't going to come tonight." His voice was pleasant enough, but she sensed an undercurrent of unease.

With a bold show of affection she let her hands snake over his chest. "Why wouldn't I want to see you?" she whispered coyly against his ear, and let her arms slip around the back of his neck.

"You know, with all that happened," he said. "I thought you'd be with Lambert tonight."

There was nervousness in his voice. What was he hiding from her? She had started to ease inside his mind when she felt someone tickling around the edges of her own. She turned. Tymmie was glaring at her, and she knew he was trying to sneak inside her head.

"Hey, Tymmie," she called, pulling away from Jerome.

She purposefully stretched up her arms, letting her top ride high in a daring show of flat tanned stomach and hipbones. Through the strobbing light she watched Tymmie study her and didn't stop her sinuous stretch until a wicked smile crept over his face. Then she knew she had convinced him she was Aura.

◄ 225 ►

Jerome grabbed her arm and yanked her back to him.

"I thought you liked a nervy girl," she teased, and moved in unhurried steps into his arms.

"The others do," he said, his anger intense.

"Don't be jealous," she whispered in a soothing tone. She didn't need his rampage of emotions getting into the mix before she found Stanton. "You're the one I like."

He didn't answer, but she tipped inside his head and felt his anger go away. His hands glided up her back to her neck, finally cupping her face for a kiss.

"I need something to drink," she said as his lips touched hers.

"Come on." He grabbed her hand and pulled her through the throng of dancers.

She glanced behind the cobweb-covered safety cables dangling from a broken beam, trying to see in the dark corner. She didn't know how long she could keep up her deception. Already a nervous tremor was building in her fingers. She needed to find Stanton quickly and leave. If he were still alive, she was confident he had to be somewhere in the factory.

When she finally saw him tied to a large vertical pipe, a hopelessness swept over her. Ropes could never hold a shape changer unless he was desperately weakened. Even in the percolating light, she could see brown rings circling his eyes.

She tried to go inside his mind to let him know she was here, but his thoughts had become an impenetrable maze. Maybe they had hurt him more than she was aware. Could he be dying?

He glanced up, sensing her presence, and his lips trembled as if he were trying to speak.

"Come on." Jerome touched her, and she drew back with a start.

"I'll wait here," she said. "Get me a Coke or some water. My mouth is dry."

He didn't seem to want to leave her, and she again sensed his mistrust.

"I promise I won't go anywhere," she coaxed.

As soon as he left her, she hurried to Stanton. She had almost reached him when someone grabbed her wrist and yanked her back. She turned sharply and stared at a huge guy with three hoops piercing his nose. His mind reached into hers for one awful moment of understanding and in a flash she knew he knew she wasn't Aura. Their thoughts melded together, each blocking the other's power, and then she rammed deeper inside him, plunging down, and just when she felt she was going to be lost forever inside his ugly emotions, she found what she had been looking for. She pulled slumber forward. His eyes closed, chin falling to his chest, and his hefty weight fell against her. She eased his giant body to the floor as a snore escaped his mouth.

She hurriedly glanced around, her fear over-taking her now. Had others seen her? She studied the shadows behind Stanton, looking for any shift in movement that might betray a shape-changing Follower. Finally she let out a sigh of relief, only she didn't have time to free Stanton now. She hurried back to the dancers and smiled when Jerome handed her a Coke. She took one sip, but her fingers felt too shaky to keep the cold can in her hand, so she gave it to a girl wearing a short see-through dress.

"Come with me," she whispered against Jerome's ear, pulling him into the corner from which she had just come, carefully using her body to block his view of the fallen guard.

When they were close to Stanton, she stopped.

Jerome looked nervously around. "We better get back with the others."

She laughed wickedly, then teased, "I thought you wanted some time alone with me."

"Initiates aren't supposed to go near Stanton," he explained, his eyes wary.

"Stanton?" she asked as if she hadn't been aware that they were only a few feet from him now. "I don't understand why we can't be here," she said, and brazenly placed his hand on her bare waist.

When she sensed his desire overcoming his fear, she gently pushed into his mind.

"Serena?" he asked suddenly as if he felt her inside his head, pulling him back from the Atrox.

He had only recently become an Initiate, but already he had surrendered his hope and dreams. His heart was too eager to please the dark one. She let her power build, then tore that darkness from his mind, hoping it would be enough to save him.

"Sorry," she whispered to him as she eased him next to the fallen guard.

Even in the dim light she could feel him looking at her, eyes wide, trying to understand.

She left Jerome sitting with a blank stare, knowing that it would take a few minutes for him to become aware, and hopefully by then she and Stanton would be gone. She dashed over to Stanton and began untying his ropes. She had the first one undone when someone grabbed her shoulders and spun her around.

Tymmie smiled down at her, his thoughts creeping into her head. She slammed her mind shut, catching him by surprise. The warrior goddess emerged and she prepared to fight. She was aware of others gathering around her, their movements slow, eyes hungry and anxious for a fray.

Abruptly the music stopped and the house

lights came on. Followers quit dancing and turned to her, their tattoos seeming iridescent now, eyes blazing yellow. Girls whooped and squealed, some dissolving into fuzzy silhouettes.

Tymmie took a step forward, guys shoving around him.

"You're outnumbered, Serena," he said. "Maybe you should call the other Daughters to come help you."

"No way." Serena stood her ground as her moon amulet shot out a flurry of blue sparks, its heat fierce against her bare skin. She could feel the energy building inside her.

"You want to do it alone?" Tymmie sneered, his eyes flashing with anticipation, and then his body began to dim, his features becoming indistinct as he faded into dark airy shade, showing off his new power as an *infidus*.

Serena's heart fell. Catty had been right all along. There was no way she could fight a horde of phantom figures.

CHAPTER TWENTY-FOUR

SERENA WAITED FOR them to attack, but they stood still, eyes focused on something behind her. She turned quickly. Stanton staggered forward, unwinding a rope from his wrist, his blue eyes piercing. Now she understood. Not one of the Followers was brave enough to be the first to test Stanton's power. But what had revived him? Had her presence somehow nourished him? The

Followers backed away in stunned silence. Without Lambert, they were no match for the Prince of Night, even in his weakened state.

Serena clasped Stanton's wrist, hoping to give him some of her strength.

"Don't look in their eyes," Stanton warned, his voice weak.

His caution came too late. Tymmie caught her glimpse, his gaze gripping hers. Suddenly the mental assault from the disloyal Followers hit her with riveting pain. She winced. The cold hypnotic feeling grew inside her head, their thoughts urging her to stay and surrender Stanton.

She clutched the moon amulet hanging around her neck. It pulsed violently against her fingers, casting an eerie glow. She held it high, feeling the hot stone transfer energy through her skin down to her bones. Maggie had told her the charm had no power of its own—it was only a symbol of her strength. But now she wondered, because suddenly an intense force jolted through her.

The air shuddered and a flash of light swept

from her. Tymmie's eyes widened as fear cut across his face. He didn't have enough time to deflect her attack. The mental hold on her dropped as an ethereal brightness shrouded him. His teeth clenched in pain, and then he smiled derisively as if to tell her he had not been hurt even though fiery embers still pulsed around his head.

She didn't think any of them would attack now, but she wasn't taking any chances. Her eyes remained dilated, expanded in savage rage, as she stayed ready to strike again. The Followers stepped back, retreating into shadows, their bodies seeming to evaporate and melt away as they changed.

"Come on." She grabbed Stanton's hand and rushed him outside.

The cool night hit her with reviving strength. Only then did she realize how terrified she had been.

"Hurry!" she yelled, kicking off her sandals. She pulled Stanton behind her and then they ran, her feet slapping over the broken concrete.

Without streetlights, the shadows between

the buildings were perfect covering for shape changers. She didn't see any movement in the tomblike blackness, but the Followers had to be nearby. And soon they would summon Lambert to join forces with them.

"Jimena!" she shouted as the bottoms of her feet hit the gravel near the railroad tracks.

In answer to her yell, a car engine revved and the beams of headlights pierced the darkness, shining brightly in her eyes.

Serena yanked open the car door, shoved Stanton into the front seat, and dove in after him.

"How'd you get him out?" Jimena asked, not bothering to hide the suspicion in her voice. She slammed her foot on the accelerator and the car blasted away, tires skidding around the corner, tailpipes roaring.

"The Followers were afraid to test Stanton's power. . . ." But even as Serena said the words, she knew something was wrong. She turned, breathless, her heart hammering, and looked out the rear window, searching for thickening shadows. Their escape had been too easy.

"It doesn't make sense that they're just letting us get away," Catty said, looking down at her moon amulet. It was glowing.

"It's got to be a trap." Vanessa's face was shining from the luster of her charm.

"Stop the car," Stanton said.

"Are you *loco*?" Jimena answered gruffly.

"Why?" Serena asked. "Do you sense an attack?"

"I need to talk to you," Stanton said in a silky voice. "In private."

"Now?" Jimena asked.

"Yes," Stanton answered.

Jimena put her foot on the brake and the car started to slow.

"Don't stop!" Serena shouted. "We're not far enough away from the Followers yet."

But the car clanked to the side of the street and parked at the curb.

"Go talk to him," Jimena urged. "It could be important."

"Don't you understand the danger?" Serena argued, her eyes watchful, inspecting the dark for an unnatural rip in the shadows that would reveal the presence of a Follower.

Stanton leaned over her and opened the car door. "Come on," he said. "Now's not the time to be stubborn."

Reluctantly Serena stepped from the car, her eyes vigilant.

Stanton folded his arms around her. "You and I are safe here. The traitors can't harm you when you're with me."

She looked up at him, wondering how he could have forgotten what had happened at the peninsula. Couldn't he sense how dangerous it was now?

"What do you need to tell me?"

"Join me," he whispered, his eyes seductive and compelling.

"Join you?" That was the last thing she had expected him to say. She shook her head and started back to the car, but he grabbed her arm, pulling her to him, his fingers tracing up her throat to her face.

"You've always known that your destiny was to betray the other Daughters," he said.

"Never," she whispered harshly. "That will never happen."

He soothed his hand over her cheek. "You're *lecta*, the one chosen by the Atrox to receive eternal life. Let it give you that gift now so we can be together forever."

She glanced back. The car door was open. She was certain the others could hear what Stanton was saying, so why weren't they getting ready to defend her?

"Jimena!" she called.

"She can't hear you," Stanton said.

"Vanessa! Catty! Tianna!" None of them turned. She stepped closer, and even in the dim light she could see their dreamy, spellbound stares. Was Stanton so powerful that he could control four minds at once?

"I have so much more power now," he whispered, drawing her back to him. "I didn't think you'd want your friends to overhear our conversation."

"If you're so strong, how did the Followers capture you?" she snapped.

"I let them," he said. "I let them take me away to keep them from harming you. I only remained their prisoner to spy out their treachery."

She felt his hand on her chest and with a hitch of her breath glanced down. He was holding Hekate's charm in his fingers.

"The dark of the moon is sacred to the witch goddess Hekate," Stanton continued. "I've always known she was part of you. And now you wear her orb. It's an omen for you to join me."

"I wear two charms," she corrected. "Both Selene and Hekate protect me." But still she wondered why he had seemed so surprised to see Hekate's circle around her neck. Did the orb mean something more than she understood?

"Think of the power you'd have if you allowed yourself," he went on. "You'd control both moonlight and darkness."

"I've already made my choice," she insisted. "You see my choice as one between weakness and power, but I see it as a choice between hope and despair."

"I know the deepest parts of you, Serena," he continued, as if he sensed her doubt. "Darkness lingers inside you from the night you stepped into the Cold Fire."

"I fell into the fire," she argued, and shuddered, remembering the bitter cold of the icy inferno.

"But you also remember how sweet it felt. Your body craves the caressing flames." His hands slid up her arms. "The way you crave my touch."

She started to pull away from him again, but he stopped her.

"Remember the fierce hunger the fire awakened inside you?" He spoke against her ear. "You loved the power. I can give that to you again."

She remembered how she had struggled to leave the fire at first and then how the icy flames had broken down her resistance and she had wanted to stay. She would be a Follower now if Jimena hadn't risked her life to save her. She glanced at her best friend, still staring blankly at the windshield.

Stanton took her into his thoughts, but

entering his mind felt somehow different from before. She recoiled from the strange snarl of memories, ones she had never seen before. Had the Followers done that to him? She tried to leave his mind, but he snagged her in a confusing network of pictures, showing her luxury and wealth.

"What real joy comes from that?" she asked, breaking from his hold. "I know the hollowness of the Atrox's promise. I've felt it before. Even its eternal life is empty, waking day after day to a dark, hopeless world. I don't want what you're offering. Anything given by the Atrox is a sham."

"You don't understand, Serena. You won't have to deal with the Atrox," he explained. "I plan to conquer it."

She pulled back with a wrench, her heart racing. "I knew Lambert wanted to overthrow the Atrox, but I didn't know you were part of it."

"Now you know. The Atrox would never have allowed us to be together," Stanton explained. "It wants to use you for its own gain because you are the key."

"You're doing it for me?" she asked, stunned,

but another doubt was building in her mind. Down at the beach he had wanted to protect the Atrox and punish the traitors. Had that only been a deception? Or was he deceiving her now?

"What?" he asked, his eyes suddenly troubled, as if he had sensed her thoughts. He tried to slip inside her head, but she blocked him.

"If that's true, then why didn't I see that you had joined with Lambert when I was in your mind?" she asked.

"I never joined Lambert," he answered. "He will be the first one I destroy after the Atrox."

She should have been able to see Stanton's rebellion when she was inside his thoughts, but she had to put that worry aside for later. Right now she had a more pressing concern. "I don't want you to do this, Stanton. A war in the underworld could harm my world."

"We'll conquer it, too," he soothed, "and rule both."

She stared at him. She had been foolhardy to risk everything to save him. She felt heartsick. How had she never sensed his unbending ambition before? Had love blinded her? She wondered now if he had always used some kind of low-grade mind control over her, planning for this day.

A soft rustling sound made her turn and look behind her. At first she only saw the shadows between the warehouses, but then jet-black silhouettes formed, pulling together into solid figures as one by one the Followers stepped from the dark, their smiles threatening and cold.

Footsteps echoed into the night and she looked down the street. Tymmie pulled Jerome, holding him roughly by the arm, and stood with the others, an ominous look on his face.

"They will join with me," Stanton assured her, his voice so disquieting now. "But I need you."

Serena looked at the menacing throng of Followers, edging closer to her, and wondered how she had been deceived so easily.

"It's your destiny to be with me," Stanton insisted.

She shook her head, trying to be brave, but her body trembled violently in his embrace.

"Don't be afraid," he soothed. "You're part of the dark now."

"I did love you, Stanton," she whispered, holding him close, her power building. She had to stop him.

"You love me still," he said, but there was no longer certainty in his voice.

"Good-bye, Stanton," she said as an overwhelming sorrow swept through her.

She was about to release her force on him when she caught a peculiar flicker in his deep blue eyes. A haze lifted, and with a jolt she realized she was gazing into Lambert's dead stare.

Within seconds the film descended again and what she had seen there was gone. Once again Stanton's beautiful, enticing eyes were looking down at her, but now she knew they were only a veil hiding Lambert's presence in Stanton's body.

Then she remembered Hekate's message. *"Leva velamen."* She said the words out loud. "Lift the veil."

Even as her power continued to increase, she

dove into Stanton's mind, squeezing through the maze that hadn't been there before. Immediately she felt Lambert trying to drive her back. Now she understood that Lambert had deceived her, not Stanton. He had been hiding inside Stanton, waiting for her to rescue him since the traitorous Followers had abducted Stanton. His plan had always been to trick her into joining forces with him. Lambert needed her power to overthrow the Atrox. He couldn't succeed without the key.

She was suddenly aware that her energy was straining, ready to release. Already flecks of prismatic lights floated in the air around her. She tried to contain her force, but without warning it rocketed from her, an invisible bolt of pure energy, and struck Stanton.

He reeled back, stunned.

"Stanton!" she cried.

Bluish arcs danced around his eyes.

"So you understand at last." Lambert spoke to her through Stanton's lips. "Now you've destroyed the very person you love."

The blue light flashed into the dark night,

and when it was gone, Stanton's body crumpled to the ground.

She fell to her knees beside him, clasping his arm, their minds melding. He could feel her sadness and she could feel his love.

He lifted a hand to touch her, his eyes fighting to stay open. "I'll miss you, Serena."

"Part of me will go with you," she whispered, tears falling down her cheeks. "I promise we'll be together again. I'll find a way."

"Too late." His hand fell to his side, and Stanton was gone.

CHAPTER TWENTY-FIVE

Hot tears ran down Serena's face, but she couldn't give in to her grief now. She had her friends to protect. She stood, wiping her eyes.

The blue radiance hovered near her and then suddenly swept toward Jerome.

"What the—?" Jerome backed away from the speeding light, his eyes wide with terror, a blue luster illuminating his face.

The light wove around him, seeming to seep in and out of his head.

Jerome's mouth opened in a despairing scream, and then he turned in a reckless attempt to escape; but the Followers caught him and the light shot inside him. His body twitched as if gripped in pain.

He was still shuddering when he turned, eyes hazy, and focused on Serena, his expression turning hard and cold. Evil pinched his handsome features until they seemed ugly and fierce.

"Do you want to see your friends destroyed also?" The voice was still Jerome's, but with a menacing timbre now.

Bitter hate rushed through Serena. She had to surrender. It was the only way to save her friends. She stood defiantly before him, nerves throbbing. "You need me to overthrow the Atrox," she said. "I'll join you, but for a price. Leave Jerome's body and let the other Daughters go unharmed, then I'll give you my amulet."

"Agreed." Jerome smiled cruelly.

Immediately Jimena slid from behind the

steering wheel across the seat and jumped out, the trance broken. Catty wrenched open the rear car door, and the others rushed to Serena.

Jimena pressed protectively in front of her, looking around. When she saw Stanton, her face froze. "What happened to Stanton?"

"Lambert was in his body," Serena began, and then told them everything. At last she nodded toward Jerome. "Now he's inside Jerome."

"Lambert?" Catty asked, her voice shaky. The last time they had fought Lambert, his power had sent Catty into another dimension.

Serena fingered her amulet, and the metal pulsed and radiated light. She took it off and started to hand it to Jerome.

Jimena stopped her. "What's with this?"

"I have to give it to Lambert. It's the only way to save all of you."

"You can't give him your amulet." Vanessa scowled. "If you do, we'll all be weakened."

Before they could stop him, Jerome snapped the charm from Serena's hand. The metal burned his flesh. He dangled it in front of Jimena and

Serena in challenge, then, laughing, held it high in triumph.

"Do you really think they'll let us go because you surrendered?" Catty asked. "They never do."

"But can't you see I had no choice?" Serena looked at the accusation in their eyes. "You would have done the same for me."

"United we had a chance," Vanessa said. "But now—"

"Now we'll still beat them," Jimena interrupted, hooking arms with Serena. "The amulet's only a symbol of Serena's power. She's still got the real stuff inside her."

"We're not giving up our friend!" Tianna shouted to Jerome, then edged closer to Serena, locking arms with her on the other side.

"You don't know Lambert's power," Catty whispered, linking up with Vanessa, her hands trembling.

"At least it's not the dark of the moon yet." Vanessa searched the sky for the comforting crescent light.

Jerome laughed. "The moon has already slid below the horizon, beginning another night. By the lunar calendar it's the dark of the moon already. No moon magic to help you now."

"Get Tymmie first," Jimena ordered.

An invisible wave hurtled from them, rushing toward Tymmie.

"Why isn't he trying to deflect it?" Catty whispered.

But as their force was about to hit him, Tymmie vanished, becoming a shadow and skating free, a plume of darkness waving in the night. Their energy exploded against the warehouse. The siding rumbled. Windows broke and glass shattered, raining on the pavement.

Serena hated the satisfied look on Jerome's face.

Followers flanked them, seeming ready to pounce.

"Try again," Vanessa whispered. "See if we can catch one by surprise."

"They're playing this like a game of dodgeball," Tianna said. "Look at one but aim at another, someone in the back. That girl with the green stars in her hair."

The Daughters locked arms again. Their power shot out with a blinding light, but before it struck the girl, she snapped back with a wicked grin, turning into a phantasm and slipping safely away. The air convulsed as their power burst into a whirlwind of sparks, twisting into the sky.

Followers stopped advancing and watched the fireworks, then turned back, some patting at the embers still falling.

Serena could feel the raw determination of her friends, but she also knew it was useless.

"Let's go after their leader," Jimena whispered.

The air split with a jolt and Jerome staggered back.

"Stop!" Serena screamed. "Don't strike Jerome."

"We have to get Lambert," Catty insisted. "The others just vanish before we can get them."

"You'll only hurt Jerome," Serena said. "It will be like my attack on Stanton. As soon as Jerome is fatally injured, Lambert will leave his body and find someone else."

"There's got to be a way," Jimena said.

They stood together, their bodies thrumming with power, and watched the Followers circling closer.

"Lambert's going to attack," Catty warned. "What should we do?"

As she spoke, Jerome lifted his hand, taking aim at Catty, then hesitated and directed his focus at Jimena. Serena lunged in front of Jimena as flames flickered from the tip of Jerome's hand. When he saw Serena in front of Jimena, he curled his fingers down and the fire bolt shot into the ground, rocking the earth. The concrete cracked and flames sprouted inside the fissures.

"Now do you see?" Serena turned and faced them. "I have to go with him."

"You can't." Jimena grabbed her hand.

"I will," Serena insisted, pulling away. "That should give you enough time to stop them."

"How?" Vanessa said.

"Maggie will be back soon," Serena answered. "She has to know a way."

Suddenly the Followers stepped aside.

"What now?" Catty asked, her voice small and baffled.

Morgan pushed through the crowd, strutting toward them, wearing tight black hot pants over fishnet hose, platform boots, and a leather jacket. Red lipstick covered her pouty lips, and thick black lines extended from the corners of her eyes. Her attitude was palpable.

"Morgan?" Vanessa started toward her, but Jimena held her back.

Morgan gave them an arrogant smile. "Call me Aura now." She smoothed her hands down her new body as if she enjoyed its feel. "You like what I got? It's spectacular, isn't it?"

"It was Morgan all along." Vanessa's eyes widened in disbelief. "You were right, Serena. Aura only wanted you to free Lambert."

"How many bodies can she possess at one time?" Tianna asked.

"As many as I want," Aura countered, her smile derisive.

"No wonder Morgan was getting spooked," Catty said.

"Now the ceremony begins." Aura brushed her fingers through her luxurious hair. "The Prince of Night has already been sacrificed, and it's time for the key." Aura held out her hand. "Come with me, Serena. You destroyed Stanton. Do you want to be responsible for the destruction of your friends as well?"

Jimena looked at Aura with barely contained fury. "Just try and take her."

"Sorry," Serena whispered to her friends, and stepped away, taking Aura's hand.

CHAPTER TWENTY-SIX

SERENA FELT A pressure against her chest. She started to touch her moon amulet but stopped. Jerome still held it. Then she remembered Hekate's circle. Her heart began to race. She glanced down. The sapphire spun within the gold, creating the soft, sweet chant of an arcane religious song. She paused and listened. The words were in ancient Greek. She translated some of the lyrics into English: "Nocturnal One, Queen of the Cosmos." She knew at once it was an ancient prayer to summon the Greek deity Hekate.

At the same moment dogs barked and howled, and the night filled with the pure scent of clean winter air.

Serena stopped and studied the Followers, all looking at her now with an apprehensive stare. Some even backed away.

She turned to Jerome. His malicious gaze flickered, and she caught a glimpse of fear. Was there something in the night more powerful than Followers and the Atrox?

The force of Hekate surged through her, and finally she understood what it meant to be the key. She no longer saw light and dark as opposites but as two joining and necessary forces. The strength of both merged inside her with an agonizing clash, but the pain was pleasant and strangely thrilling as it molded her into the goddess she was destined to become.

An insolent smile slipped across her face and she sauntered toward Jerome.

"You said it was the dark of the moon

already," she said. "Followers are most powerful then." She paused and added, "But so am I."

She looked at the Followers who had stayed. The force of their thoughts came at her in an invisible wave. Her heart pounded with new energy. She was untouched by their mental attack.

"From my darkest moment comes my strongest," she whispered as a blinding spike of purple light shot from the stone and split through the night.

The Followers tried to merge into darkness and escape as before, but the lavender light spread out, absorbing shadows and releasing them in glowing blues and magentas. Now the Followers had no dark in which to hide. They struggled against the radiant plum color, unable to repulse the true power of the night. The orchid beams seemed to heat their bodies, causing a curious chemical reaction that made their skin gleam and burn.

"Wow," Tianna said under her breath, awestruck, and ran up next to Serena. "You've got to show me how to do that."

"Where'd you get that power?" Catty asked, her arm locking automatically with Tianna and Vanessa's.

"From the dark." Serena stopped as the intense pressure in her chest continued to build. The Followers sensed another assault and edged back, some turning and taking flight, their footsteps echoing behind them.

Serena faced Lambert now. He stared at her vindictively through Jerome's eyes.

Power surged in her brain again, her head throbbing as the fierce power of an enraged goddess charged through her. Her surroundings blurred, and at last her concentration became complete. Hekate was taking over her body, eager to battle Lambert.

Before Lambert could respond with an attack of his own, Serena struck, her body swaying from the thrust of the energy leaving her.

Jerome staggered back, and she used that moment to enter Lambert's spirit with her mind control. She wrestled with him, trying to drive him from Jerome, but suddenly she felt the consciousness of someone else trapped within his ego. Her mental hold broke and she fell back into her own body.

"Stanton!" she yelled. Could Lambert have stolen Stanton's spirit, absorbing his life force and using it for his own?

Jimena embraced her. "What did you see?"

"Look!" Catty pointed.

The blue light hovered around Jerome's eyes, undecided, then streaked away. Jerome fell to the ground, and when he blinked, his eyes looked confused.

"Stanton's imprisoned inside Lambert." Serena knew with certainty that what she said was true. She had to do something quickly. She had gone inside so many minds, so why couldn't she go inside the light? It was the same, wasn't it? A combination of thoughts and memories, the core of an evil soul.

"Don't do it," Jimena warned, seeming to sense what she had planned. "He'll trap you inside."

"Too late," Serena whispered, her energy already sweeping from her body.

With the force of her mind she cut into the light, slicing through a tangle of brutal thoughts, and plunged deeper, searching for Stanton. She felt sickened by the depth of hatred in Lambert's mind.

As she fell deeper, doubts began to wear down her confidence. What would happen if she couldn't find Stanton? Could she even find her way out again?

At last she located his spirit. *Stanton!* She didn't wait for his reply. She had been in his mind too many times not to recognize his entity. She brought him into her power and started to leave, but another force blocked her and pulled at her like a riptide, sucking her back. She tried to fight it, but the harder she struggled, the stronger it became.

Suddenly she was traveling backward, falling at breakneck speed in a spiral toward Lambert's core. Her mind's eye became clouded, and even with total concentration she could no longer get her bearing. She sensed that if she reached the middle of this maze, she would never be able to find her way out again.

Without warning she stopped. She cried out as her feet hit solid ground. She was solid and whole again. When had that happened? Lambert had trapped her inside a memory. She looked around, her stomach still queasy, and with a gasp stepped back. Her heart thundered in her chest and her legs began shaking. She stood on the shelf of a rocky precipice.

The vertical incline of the jagged summit above her looked impossible to climb, and the sheer drop below made her dizzy. She swerved back, pressing against the cold bedrock behind her. She was terrified of heights. Was she going to spend an eternity here?

Finally she steadied her nerves and forced herself to lean forward again. She stole a glance into the canyon below, looking for a trail or pathway down to the floor. A bluish fog rolled lazily at the bottom of the ravine. It seemed more like a transparent veil than haze.

Her breath caught and she bit her lip. A

veil! Now she understood the true meaning of Hekate's message.

"*Leva velamen*," she chanted. "Lift the veil."

The veil she needed to lift was the one covering her own eyes. She was imprisoned in an illusion created by Lambert. All she had to do was break through the fantasy world caging her, but how?

The Daughters had once used pain to awaken Catty from a hypnotic state when a Regulator had entrapped her in a dream. Serena remembered that when Jimena had hit her, the trance had broken and Catty had been released from the spell.

Serena braced herself against the crevasse wall, then slapped her arm again and again, hoping the stinging would make this surreal world shatter.

When nothing happened, she took a step forward and peered over the ledge to the rocky canyon floor. The drop didn't look like an illusion. If she jumped, she would plunge to her death. But it had to be a deception.

"Leva velamen," she whispered.

She clasped Stanton's life force tightly inside her mind, then took a deep breath and dove into the abyss.

CHAPTER TWENTY-SEVEN

*S*ERENA HIT THE pavement hard and her mind spun back to reality. A tooth chipped and the taste of blood filled her mouth. She grinned up at Jimena in spite of the pain filling her, then rested her cheek in the street grime. She breathed in the fine particles of automobile exhaust, the smells of industry hydrocarbons and motor oil, then listened to the distant whir of tires speeding down the freeway, feeling overjoyed to be back in Los Angeles.

Jimena grabbed her arm and pulled her up. Serena's legs felt too shaky to support her weight, but she couldn't keep the silly smile off her face. "I'm back."

"Lambert trapped you, didn't he?" Jimena asked. "You were standing there with a blank stare and didn't react to anything we said."

Serena nodded, stretching her back against the throbbing ache in her spine.

"You didn't even flinch when I slugged you," Tianna said with a devilish look. "They told me to do it."

"That worked on me," Catty said sheepishly.

"It was weird the way you kept slapping your arm." Vanessa brushed the dirt from Serena's cheek. "Are you all right?"

Serena wiped at the blood on her lips. "Yeah, I'm feeling great."

"Then all of a sudden you looked like you were diving into a swimming pool." Catty waved her arms, mimicking Serena's fall. "We tried to stop you."

"I was diving off a cliff again. Lambert must have known how much I'm afraid of heights." Then her head whipped around. "Where's Stanton?"

She turned as he rose up on his elbows. His *thank you* drifted sweetly across her mind. She helped him stand.

"Look out!" Vanessa shouted.

Serena looked up as a blue stroke of lightning shrieked toward them. She shoved Stanton out of its path and dove after him. The bolt struck a mesh fence with a terrible rattle. Thunder crackled, vibrating through the ground. A hot billow of air puffed out from the impact, smelling of molten metal. The chain links and posts glowed red.

Stanton jumped up, grabbed Serena's arm, and lifted her against him. Together they faced Lambert's spirit and his advancing garrison of Followers.

Their powers merged into a tremendous force.

Now, Stanton whispered across her mind, and their combined energy sped into the night, exploding in a blinding flash.

The Followers hesitated, but Tymmie roused them into formation and they continued forward, following Lambert's essence, bobbing above them in the blue sphere.

This time when Stanton and Serena released their force, it split through the blue light. The glowing globe burst into a fireball. Flames looped out from the blaze like flares in the sun's corona.

The Followers stopped suddenly, terror in their eyes, and watched the bits of fire cascading around them. They all turned and ran away.

"Should we go after them?" Tianna asked.

"I don't think we need to," Serena said. "The Atrox will send Regulators to destroy them."

Vanessa shuddered. "Do you think Lambert is really gone?"

"No!" Aura screamed, her hair wreathing around her head as if caught in a sudden upward breeze.

Jimena turned. "We forgot about Aura."

Suddenly wind screeched from Morgan's body in a fury, gathering strength. It rotated into a whirlwind, picking up dust and debris. The rubbish-filled funnel cloud churned faster, spinning and stretching, and then disappeared as rapidly as it had come. Dirt, fast-food wrappers, aluminum cans, and dried weeds rained down on them.

Serena ran to Morgan. "Are you all right?"

Morgan looked at her blankly, her hands patting her chest as if she were searching for her amulets to ward off evil sprits.

"Kind of late for good-luck charms, isn't it?" Catty teased, and draped an arm around her. "Do you have any clue at all about what just happened?"

"Stay away from me, you freak!" Morgan said, and jerked away from Catty.

Catty shrugged. "Sorry you feel that way." Then she looked at Tianna. "Aura should have kept her. They were a perfect match."

Morgan turned back and glared at Catty, then climbed into Jimena's car, her fingers combing through her tangled hair.

"She should be more upset," Serena said to Jimena.

Jimena nodded. "We better watch her for a while. She might have turned back."

"At least we got rid of Lambert and Aura." Vanessa walked over to the car.

Serena caught Stanton's doubt. "What?" she asked.

"We're not rid of them," he said softly. "We only stopped them for now."

"How can Lambert have survived that?" Vanessa asked.

"His entity lives." Stanton scanned the black sky like someone searching for a falling star. "He was a member of the Inner Circle who wore the Phoenix crest. So he's more enduring than an Immortal."

"Let's go." Jimena opened the car door and fell in behind the steering wheel. She looked worn out. "Get Jerome. We're out of here."

Serena looked around. Jerome was standing in the street, looking around in a daze.

She took his arm and walked him over to the

car. She curled into his mind to hide his memories of what had happened. Then she eased back out, took her moon amulet out of his hands, and walked away.

She placed her moon amulet around her neck and looked at the shadows, wondering when the battle would continue, but then she remembered Jimena's premonition. The first part had come true. She had joined with Stanton to fight Followers who wanted to overthrow the Atrox. Did that mean the second part of her vision would also come true? She glanced at Stanton. Would she choose to remain with him forever?

"Come on," Jimena said, tapping her fingers impatiently on the steering wheel. "Let's go."

"I'll catch you later," Serena answered, slamming the car door.

CHAPTER TWENTY-EIGHT

SERENA AND STANTON stood in the street, waiting for the car to drive away. When the taillights disappeared, Stanton wrapped his arms around her and kissed her gently. A pleasant ache rushed through her. Everything that had happened over the past few days seemed so distant. All that existed now was Stanton and the way he was making her feel.

perhaps. But now, unlike the other Daughters, Serena had a third choice. She could become a goddess of the dark.

"I've decided. I'm going to—"

He touched her lips with the tip of his finger to silence her, then, pressing her tightly against him, they dissolved into shadow.

Don't miss the next

DAUGHTERS OF THE MOON book,

The choice

BREATHLESS, JIMENA SLOWED her steps and joined the crowd walking from the public parking areas toward the Staples Center. The huge gathering was like a musical melting pot. Headbangers, hip-hoppers, and punk-rockers strolled together, some singing, their energy high and contagious, and seeming to vibrate into the air.

She passed guys selling T-shirts with the band's picture on the front. Other vendors held posters and glow sticks in their hands.

A horn honked in quick beats and then someone called her name. "Jimena!"

She turned.

Collin waved from behind the wheel of his utility van and swung the vehicle to the curb. He

"Stanton . . ." She started to ask him how Lambert had caught him, but he closed her mouth with another kiss. She loved the feel of his body against her.

"I love you, Serena," he said at last. "Be with me."

Her breath caught. "I can't join your world."

He shook his head. "I'm not talking about joining forces for some nefarious plot; I'm talking about being together."

Before she was even aware, he seeped inside her mind and she knew he was sorting through her secret fantasies. He smiled at her attempt to hide her private daydreams. She bit her lower lip when he saw how much she desired him.

He lifted her chin. "Don't be shy. I have the same dreams about you. Let me show you."

Her heart raced as a fanfare of dazzling pictures spun before her mind's eye.

"See?" He smiled, knowing that she had seen how much he cared about her.

"But it's too dangerous," she said at last.

"Regulators will destroy us both if we stay together."

"No," he answered, caressing her cheek. "Since I went back to the Atrox, my power is stronger than it ever has been. I command the Regulators now, and nothing is denied me, not even you."

Serena realized that she had been using the danger as an excuse. It was easier than making a decision. She stared into Stanton's eyes. Maybe she had always been destined to be like Hekate, a goddess of dark, but was that so bad? It was during dark times that people most needed help from the divine. She understood that now.

"There never was a night that didn't end," she whispered.

Stanton looked at her. "You have to make a choice."

She nodded. Her seventeenth birthday was quickly approaching, and then she had to choose. She could lose her powers and her memory of what she had once been, or she could disappear and become something else, a guardian spirit, looked angry and tired. She stepped to the van as the automatic window rolled down.

"I don't have time—"

"Get in the car." He leaned over and opened the door for her. He had dark circles under his eyes. "I'll give you a ride to the center."

Reluctantly, she climbed in and buckled her seat belt.

"I've been looking for you since last night." He eased into the slow-moving traffic. "You should have told someone where you were going. I was worried something had happened to you. Everyone was."

"Right," she snapped. "If you were so worried, then why did you break up with me?"

"You're the one who always acted like the relationship wasn't important, not me," he answered defensively.

His head whipped around. "What?"

"Even Friday night. You didn't seem happy to see me. All you wanted to do was talk to Serena."

"You had already found your girlie-girl to replace me!" Jimena's voice was tight with anger. "I saw you with her at Corrine's party."

◄   2   ►

"Melissa?"

"I don't know her name." Jimena folded her arms over her chest. "And I don't care."

"You're jealous of Melissa?"

"I'm not *celosa* of anybody."

"Melissa is Hunter's younger sister. She just started going out and she's shy. I was trying to give her some confidence. I'm not interested in her." Then the anger returned to his voice. "Not like your interest in Robert!"

"Robert? I don't like Robert," Jimena shot back.

Collin jerked the steering wheel. The car lunged to the side of the road and jarred to a stop. Horns honked in protest. He grabbed Jimena's hand and pulled her to him. She hadn't anticipated his touch and a shock of adrenaline rushed through her. His fingers curled under her chin and he made her look into his eyes.

She glanced up at him, trying not to give in. His breath caressed her face, his lips inches from hers now.

He looked down at her tenderly. "I couldn't have any romantic interest in her because I'm in love with you."

Her lower lip trembled and she tried to push back tears. "I was going to tell you how I felt at the sleep-over tonight, but you broke up with me."

"Tell me."

"I think I'm falling in love with you." The words were out and she felt totally exposed.

His hand brushed over her cheek and he kissed her lightly.

"I'm sorry," she whispered.

"I never wanted to break up with you," he said. "But you always act so tough. I thought you didn't care. Then when we did break up, it seemed like it was what you wanted."

Abruptly, she pulled away from him and wiped the tears from her cheeck. "It's too late now." She opened the car door.

He looked surprised. "Where are you going?"

She jumped out. "There's no time left," she yelled over her shoulder and started pushing wildly through the crowd. She had to get to the Staples Center. She didn't even know who the traitor was yet and she had to stop that Daughter from summoning the Atrox.